Moonstone Angel

Moonstone Landing Series
Novella

by
Meara Platt

DRAGONBLADE
PUBLISHING, INC.

ARE YOU SIGNED UP FOR DRAGONBLADE'S BLOG?

You'll get the latest news and information on exclusive giveaways, exclusive excerpts, coming releases, sales, free books, cover reveals and more.

Check out our complete list of authors, too!

No spam, no junk. That's a promise!

Sign Up Here

www.dragonbladepublishing.com

~∞~

Dearest Reader;

Thank you for your support of a small press. At Dragonblade Publishing, we strive to bring you the highest quality Historical Romance from some of the best authors in the business. Without your support, there is no 'us', so we sincerely hope you adore these stories and find some new favorite authors along the way.

Happy Reading!

CEO, Dragonblade Publishing

.

Garden of Light
Garden of Dragons
Garden of Destiny
Garden of Angels

The Farthingale Series
If You Wished For Me (A Novella)

The Lyon's Den Series
Kiss of the Lyon
The Lyon's Surprise
Lyon in the Rough

Pirates of Britannia Series
Pearls of Fire

De Wolfe Pack: The Series
Nobody's Angel
Kiss an Angel
Bhrodi's Angel

Also from Meara Platt
Aislin
All I Want for Christmas

Chapter One

Moonstone Landing
Cornwall, England
August 1815

"DO NOT FORCE me to break down your door!" Rowan, Duke of Strathmore growled, dearly wishing to throttle the irritating young woman on the other side of it. She, namely one Miss Angel, was laughing at him from her position of safety, while he stood in front of this surprisingly quaint cottage in the seaside village of Moonstone Landing and demanded to be let in.

The village was nestled in a cozy harbor in the middle of nowhere along the coast of Cornwall, and he was quite put out that the wretched girl had forced him to leave London, track her all the way here, and was now refusing to allow him entrance.

Never mind that the place appeared to hold some charm, and he might have enjoyed a visit under other circumstances.

The point was, he did not wish to be here now.

Yet here he was, being perfectly reasonable, while the girl laughed.

At *him*, of all people.

She'd slammed the door in his face, as well.

Only a madwoman would ever do such a thing to a duke with his wealth and power. "You have to the count of three, Miss Angel."

Devil is what she ought to be called.

And now a crowd was gathering behind him as he stood in the glow of the afternoon sun, a strengthening sea breeze ruffling his hair. Amid their chuckles, he could also hear the whoosh of waves breaking along the nearby beach and the distant clang of harbor bells.

Those bells were growing more insistent as the wind stiffened. "Miss Angel, this is your last warning."

"I am quaking in my boots, Your Grace," she replied with unbridled amusement. "Welcome home, by the way. Your grandmother is very proud of her war hero grandson. So am I, not that you give a fig about my feelings."

Gad, the girl was irritating.

And why should he care anything for her feelings? "London is my home, not Moonhole…whatever you call this Godforsaken place…and why is my grandmother with you when she has a perfectly suitable residence in Mayfair's Ridley Square?"

"Because Ridley Square, as lovely as that section of London might be, is not livable at this time of year. The air is wet, dirty, and choking, as you well know. It is terrible for your grandmother's lung condition. Stop pounding on my door."

He banged on it again for good measure. "Open up. I will not ask politely again."

"You call that polite? Oh, very well. I suppose we've provided enough entertainment for my neighbors." He heard the click of the latch, and in the next moment, the door groaned open just a crack. Big, hazel eyes peered back at him, causing his heart to momentarily hitch. "Will you promise not to shout at me?"

Her voice, when not muffled behind the thick oak, was soft and lilting.

Gad, this was Miss Angel?

He'd only caught a glimpse of her before she tore into the house and slammed the door in his face, but he saw her clearly now. Her eyes were beautiful and so was her impudent smile. Unruly auburn curls framed her lovely face and those amber-green orbs sparkled with mirth.

He gritted his teeth, now quite impatient. "I was never shouting at you."

"Growling very loudly, then. And you prowled up the garden path like a jungle cat determined to eat its prey. You frightened me."

Lord, she was having him on.

She did not sound frightened in the least. "First you shut me out and now you mock me. Who is the wronged one here?"

"Oh, all right. Do come in, Your Grace. But I will toss you out on your ear if you misbehave."

"Me?" He stared down at the girl, wanting to be angry with her and at the same time kiss her because she had the most beautiful mouth he had ever seen on a woman. Obviously, he had lost his mind. "Where is my grandmother?"

"You are growling at me again. Stop doing that. She is napping, although I do not know how she could have missed hearing all the noise you made." She stepped aside to allow him entrance and watched as his gaze swept across the parlor to give it a quick inspection. "Does my home meet with your approval? I hope you find it more to your liking than you find me."

She had an annoyingly sarcastic mouth, which he still—to his continued annoyance—wanted to kiss.

If only she were not such an acerbic, irreverent thing. "This is *your* home?"

She sighed and invited him to take a seat. "Yes, why do you ask? Or have your sisters, and that horrid woman who will soon be your betrothed, been filling your head with lies?"

He chose to remain standing and, instead, leaned a shoulder against the mantel of her unlit hearth. "Lady Yvonne is not a horrid woman. It is one thing to insult me, but to now—"

"Oh, spare me the indignation." She rolled her eyes. "I know she is considered a diamond of the first water, and men fall besotted at her feet. I thought you would be more discerning, but I see you are as foolish as the rest of her suitors. She wants you for your rank and deep pockets, you know. Your good looks are a point in your favor, but she would have married you even if you looked like a toad."

"For pity's sake, Miss Angel. Are you always this forthcoming with your opinions? Even when they are neither requested nor welcome? You are doing nothing to win my favor."

"I know, but why do you care? I am just the untrustworthy chit who absconded with your grandmother, and I probably stole something valuable while making my escape. What was it those three accused me of stealing? An item of your grandmother's jewelry? Or the family silver?"

He arched an eyebrow. "It was a diamond necklace."

She laughed and shook her head. "I suppose if I were to steal a thing, it would have to be the best to make it worth my while. One of the Strathmore family heirlooms?"

He nodded.

"Truly? They go straight for one's throat, don't they? Well, your grandmother will tell you the truth...unlike those three. Do have a seat, won't you? My housekeeper will bring in refreshments shortly. Will you have tea? I'm afraid I don't have anything stronger than sherry to offer you. I bought a bottle for your grandmother since she likes a small glass of it before retiring to bed."

"Tea will do. Just try not to lace it with vinegar...or arsenic," he said, a smile finally escaping his lips. He'd never believed that tripe about her being a thief, for what criminal of any merit takes a necklace and a grandmother? It did not appear as though his grandmother was being held hostage either.

She returned his smile with a warm one of her own. "You are quite safe with the tea, I assure you. But my housekeeper is not the best cook. I would eat Mildred's scones with extreme caution. However, you will be relieved to know we've ordered in our week's supply of tea cakes from Mrs. Halsey's shop on the High Street. Her cakes and pies are quite delicious, and you may munch on them to your heart's content."

"Tell me, Miss Angel. Why did you bring my grandmother here?" There were no bars on the windows and doors, and this cottage was situated among other pleasant homes within the village of Moonstone Landing—yes, he knew what the town was called. All of these nicely maintained houses stood upon a hill overlooking the sea.

She sank onto the slightly faded sofa, the sturdy damask fabric no doubt lightened by the sun shining in through the windows. She had those windows open now to allow in the afternoon breeze, which carried the scent of brine from the sea and also a trace of honeysuckle from her garden.

Her expression turned more somber. "She asked me to do it, as sort of a…"

"A dying wish?" He held back the ache that caught painfully in his throat. "My sisters told me of the string of doctors marching in and out of her home these past few months, trying to heal her."

"Yes, London's top medical men poking and prodding her until your grandmother grew weary of them and would not let them near her anymore."

"How serious is it?"

She pursed her lips, that expression alone revealing all he needed to know. But he waited to hear her out, wanting her confirmation. "From what I gather, she does not have much longer to…I'm sorry, I cannot bring myself to say the words. This is why she chased the doctors away. If she is to not see another day, she would rather it happened in peace."

"I see."

"London was awful for her." She took a deep, shaky breath and continued. "They bled her. Stuck leeches all over her body. Bruised her delicate skin so that her arms and legs were a solid wall of yellowish purple. They gave her horrid concoctions to drink."

His heart was now in utter torment, for he had not been there to help his grandmother in her time of need. But his services had been required at Waterloo, and he could not have refused to fight while the fate of Europe remained hanging in the balance. "It must have been awful for her."

"It was. She'd finally had enough and asked me to bring her to my home. I grew up in Moonstone Landing and often spoke of my pleasant life here. She wanted to see it for herself, and I could not find it in my heart to deny her. So off we went. The sun and clean air have helped restore her spirits, and she does not appear to be in pain beyond the aches expected of an elderly person."

He frowned. "That is all well and good, but this idyllic summer adventure cannot last. What did you think to do when the real pain started?"

"We have an excellent doctor here, Your Grace. He comes by to look in on her every day. His name is Dr. Hewitt, and he will answer any of your questions. He is quite knowledgeable. Please do not think I take Duchess Anne's condition lightly. But also know she is happy here, as you will see once you speak to her."

"She belongs back in London with—"

"She belongs where she is happiest. That is for her to decide, not you. I know you are quite an important person and used to people jumping to your commands. But I will not do that. Nor will I let you take your grandmother against her will."

"Me? You are the one who abducted her." He should have been angered by her impertinence, but there was something in what she said. Having experienced too many years on a battlefield, he appreciated a person's right to die in peace more than most people would.

"Stop spouting that nonsense your sisters and that woman you think is a diamond have told you. She needs your support and understanding more than ever now." Miss Angel clasped her hands together and began to wring them. "Yours especially. You see, I truly believe you are the only one in your family who loves her and the only one she trusts. The others…they're just waiting for her to die."

"You do not think my sisters care for her?"

She sighed. "You will be angry with me again, but I must speak plainly. No, they care for no one but themselves. Duchess Anne could not bear the way they came around and hovered over her like vultures. They thought she could not hear them as they dug through her belongings and chose what they wanted to take. If that diamond necklace is truly missing, then I suggest you question them about it. They're probably fighting over it between themselves as we speak."

His heart tugged, knowing she spoke the truth. Joan and Ellen were his older half-sisters, sharing the same father but different mothers. His was the second wife who had given their father an heir, namely himself. Both sisters had married well, yet despite having comfortable lives, there remained a mean-spirited pettiness to them he never understood.

Was the beautiful Lady Yvonne cast from the same mold?

He did not like to think he had been so easily fooled. Then again, after all those years on the battlefield, he may have been too quick to make up for lost time. As duke, it was his duty to marry and sire the next generation of heirs. Why not choose the loveliest debutante London society had to offer and be done with it?

It had seemed logical, at first.

Perhaps not so much now.

"Ah, here is your housekeeper," he said, easing away from the mantel as the sturdy, middle-aged woman wheeled in a laden tea cart.

"Mildred, will you please let Duchess Anne know her grandson is here, and we are to have our afternoon tea." When the woman bustled off, Miss Angel turned to him with a wry smile. "I would have gone to wake her myself but was afraid you'd think we would run out the back way to escape you. Have a seat, Your Grace. She'll be out shortly. Would you care for some lemon cake?"

"Just tea for me." He took the chair facing hers and glanced beyond to peer at the narrow staircase.

"Oh, she's not up there. I've set up her bedchamber on this main floor in what used to be my father's study. She gets around well enough in this part of the house. I have a pushchair for her when we go on our outings."

"She goes out?"

Miss Angel cast him another of her wry smiles. "She is not my prisoner. We go out whenever weather permits."

"Where do you take her?"

She shrugged. "Sometimes down to the harbor to watch the boats sail in and out. Sometimes to Mrs. Halsey's tearoom for her favorite apricot pie. Yesterday, we took a stroll along the beach promenade. She cannot go down to the beach, of course. Her chair would get stuck in the sand. But she enjoys being near it, watching the tide roll in and out. Sometimes we spot dolphins and, on rare occasions, a whale. Your Grace, what do you intend to do? Can we not resolve this before she comes out of her bedchamber?"

"No, Miss Angel. I need to see her for myself."

To his surprise, she gave no protest. "Very well—but look at her with an open mind. You'll see she needs to be here a little while longer. All I ask is that you think of her and not of your own convenience."

He took a sip of his tea and then set down his cup. "And if I allow her to stay, then what of me?"

She had just cut herself a slice of the lemon cake and was about to take a bite but put her fork down. "What do you mean?"

"Where shall you put me?"

She laughed. "I could dig a hole and plant you in my garden. What are you talking about? You cannot seriously mean to stay here. First of all, I haven't invited you. Nor will I. It isn't proper."

"Then where do you propose I stay?"

"I don't see any reason for you to remain, but if you must…there's a lovely place called the Kestrel Inn on the High Street opposite the schoolhouse."

"I've seen it. They have repairs going on at the moment. I will not be awakened every morning to someone hammering at my head."

"Oh, yes. They are expanding the inn in expectation of an influx of visitors to the area. We are becoming quite popular with your society set. Well, the Three Lions Tavern also has rooms available."

"I am not taking up residence in a tavern."

"Too low for Your Loftiness? The Duke of Malvern has a beautiful home atop the cliffs overlooking the village. I'm sure he will let you in…assuming you don't pound on his door and growl at him."

"Malvern has a residence here?" He had not realized his friend Cain St. Austell had settled here.

She nodded. "You are not the only lofty personage in town, you know. However, I am not certain he is in residence at the moment. I don't suppose it matters. You are a duke and will be welcomed into anyone's home, especially that of a fellow duke, whether he is there or not. Isn't there some unwritten rule that dukes look out for each other?"

"No, there is not and has never been such a thing." He slapped his hands to his thighs. "If my grandmother is here, then this is where I shall stay. It is settled."

Miss Angel shot to her feet, her lovely eyes blazing. "You cannot. And where am I to put your valet?"

"I did not bring him with me. This may stun you, but I am quite capable of pulling up my own trousers or putting an elegant knot in my cravat." He rose as well, knowing he stood a full head taller and was far bigger than this impertinent baggage. "I can and I will stay here. You dragged my grandmother halfway across the south of

England, now deal with the consequences."

"But I have nowhere to put you."

"That is your problem, not mine." He knew he was infuriating her, but it felt good to give her back a little of her own. After all, it was because of her bright idea that he had spent not more than a night back in London before dashing across England to come here. To add to the indignity, he would likely end up sleeping on the floor.

Well, he'd endured far worse on the Continent under brutal battle conditions.

She tipped her pert chin in the air. "I shall speak to your grand-mother about this."

"Speak to whomever you wish. It will do you no good. I shall have my way, as I do in all things." Spending a few weeks in Cornwall in the summer would not be so bad, especially in her company.

Lord, she was a pretty thing.

Not that he would ever admit it to her.

"Are we in agreement, Miss Angel?"

"Are you deluded? I will never agree to us residing in such close quarters. You really ought to take yourself off to London. The lovely Lady Yvonne must be missing your full pockets terribly."

"Gad, do you never stop being impertinent? I am not leaving with-out my grandmother." And that was another thing—he ought to be furious with the girl for insulting Lady Yvonne, the woman he had thought to marry. Well, he had been imprudent in rushing to that decision. No harm done since he'd said nothing yet to Yvonne. Nor would he see her for another few weeks, perhaps as long as an entire month, depending on how long he decided to remain here.

He would have plenty of time to give this marriage business more thought.

One thing for certain, he was never going to marry someone like Miss Angel, this devil of a girl, even if she did look delicious.

The two of them were too busy glowering at each other to notice his grandmother enter the parlor. "Cara, how lovely," she said, startling both of them. "I see you've met my grandson."

The girl's lips stretched in a wry smile. "He is hard to overlook."

"I know. Isn't he impossibly handsome?"

Chapter Two

"IMPOSSIBLE IS RIGHT," Cara muttered, trying not to soften toward this insufferable clot of a duke. Well, he was handsome as blazes, but no one would ever pry that admission from her lips while there was breath left in her.

How dare he think to take up residence in her home over her objections?

But her heart did melt as she watched him turn achingly tender toward Duchess Anne, for she was the woman who had raised him after his own mother had died in childbirth. Soon afterward, his father had died. Cara had been told the entire story and could see how much love flowed between them.

Drat, how could she hate the insufferable man now?

"Are you feeling rested, Duchess Anne?" she asked.

Oh, she looked so fragile. Yet, ever beautiful.

"Rested and happy as a butterfly now that I am in the company of my two favorite people."

"Grandmama, have a seat." The duke's voice was gentle and deeply resonant as he led her to the spot on the sofa Cara had just vacated. "Would you like a cushion for your back? Are you comfortable?"

"Thank you, dear boy. I am. Cara, will you be so kind as to do the honors and pour me a cup of tea?"

"Of course." She knew how the duke's grandmother liked her tea and also knew the cake she liked best, so she set a slice of lemon cake on her plate.

"It is so good to see you, Rowan. I knew you would come after me. Did I not tell you he would, Cara?"

"Yes, you did," she said, casting her a soft smile. "But I did not expect him to blow in like a gale-force wind."

His grandmother laughed. "This is the only way he knows how to be. Blame it on his ducal upbringing and his years of military command. He expects everything to be in tip-top shape and thinks anything can be fixed by barking orders. Alas, it cannot be. My dear boy, as you will have noticed, I am not well. Such are the ravages of age."

"No, Grandmama. You are as beautiful to me as ever." He sank into the seat beside her and took her frail hand.

She cast him a doting smile. "I have a request of you, my dear."

He nodded. "Anything for you."

"Be kind to Cara. She is only doing as I instructed."

He arched a dark eyebrow, not looking particularly pleased. "Kind? She slammed the door in my face."

Cara tried to stifle a laugh, but it came out as a snort.

She hastily put a cup of tea to her lips to cover up her mirth.

He fixed his magnificent gaze on her, quite living up to his reputation as a rogue who melted hearts. "What do you say, Miss Angel? Shall we call a truce?"

"I did not realize we were at war."

Truly, he was handsome. Dark, wavy hair that was neatly trimmed and beginning to gray ever so slightly at the temples. Yet, he could not be more than thirty years old. Likely, not even that. Perhaps the strain of war had added a certain appealing character to his face and brought on that attractive dusting of gray in his hair.

His silvery eyes captured her as did his engaging smile. "We were at war, and you were kicking my arse in battle."

"I'll try to be more gentle in the future, Your Grace. I do hope we shall be friends. You may call me Cara if you wish. Your grandmother does."

His broad shoulders and muscled arms flexed magnificently beneath the fine cut of his jacket as he pondered her offer a moment. "Cara…it is a lovely name. It means 'dear one' in Spanish."

She grinned at him. "Try not to choke on it. I know I rile you, and you do not like me."

He cast her another devastating smile. "That is not so, Miss Angel…Cara. You are taking care of my grandmother, and she obviously adores you. There must be something about you to like. I'm sure I shall figure it out eventually."

His grandmother chuckled. "Rowan, do not tease the dear girl."

He held up his hands in mock surrender. "I shall be on my best behavior while sleeping under her roof. I promise."

Her teacup rattled as she set it down and gazed from him to Cara with her mouth agape. Then a soft smile spread across her lips. "Dear boy, you are staying here? When was this decided?"

"Just now. It is all settled. I am to remain here with you until you are ready to return to London. Grandmama, you really should not be so far away from the family or your doctors."

"Family," she said with a dismissive snort. "I could no longer abide to have them around, sifting through my belongings and frowning at me because I was taking too long to die. This is why I came here, to escape them all."

"I'm sorry they made you feel this way. I know Joan and Ellen are not warm by nature."

His grandmother patted his hand. "Your sisters are condescending creatures, just as their mother was. But I ought not speak ill of the dead. Your mother was an entirely different matter. She was a love match for your father, and we all adored her. Your poor father never recovered from her loss."

14

Cara picked up the teapot and held it over her cup. "Duchess Anne, would you care for more tea?"

"Yes, my dear. That will be lovely." She turned to her grandson with a grin. "This is Cara's subtle way of drawing me out of this grim conversation. Very well, let's speak of happier topics. Where is Rowan to sleep?"

Cara coughed. "We haven't figured that part out yet. You occupy the converted study, and there are only the two bedchambers upstairs. He cannot possibly sleep in a room that close to mine."

The oaf was grinning at her, obviously enjoying her discomfort.

She cleared her throat and continued. "I'll have to sleep down here on the sofa. It is the only solution I can think of. Your grandson can then have the entire upstairs to himself."

His grandmother nodded. "Yes, that is workable. It will not be uncomfortable for you at all to curl up right here."

"I'll sleep here," the duke said, patting the well-padded seat. "There is no need for me to put Cara out."

"No, Your Grace. You'll never fit. You are too big. It will be no inconvenience for me."

He regarded her with some surprise.

It was her turn to grin. "I am not always as sour as lemons. Since you will not go away, this seems to be the best arrangement. Of course, I will need a few hours each day to attend to myself in the privacy of my own bedchamber, but we can easily work out a schedule between us. Now, let's take care of the practicalities. Have you brought clothes? And where is your horse? He'll have to be properly stabled."

"I noticed the Kestrel Inn has a fine stable beside it. I've placed Ares there and left my bags in the care of the ostler. I'll grab them now, assuming you will not slam the door in my face again."

"No more door slamming, I promise," she said, fighting the urge to warm to him. "At least, not until the next time you irk me."

His smile was softer toward her now. "I am always on my best behavior when my grandmother is around."

"And when she is not?"

"I have no answer for that yet. I've never met anyone quite like you, Cara…and I do not mean it as a compliment."

She laughed. "Ah, yes. You like your ladies to be biddable and doting on you. No independent thoughts. No challenge to your authority."

"If I am to be husband to one of them, they ought to respect me. But I'd like them to be more interesting than a wedge of cheese."

"Ah, that is quite a standard you've set for the woman you shall marry."

He joined her in a chuckle. "I've expressed myself badly. Perhaps it is because I do not know yet what I want."

"However, you do know that it cannot be anyone like me."

"Cara, you already have my head spinning, and I've not spent more than five minutes with you. If you were my wife, I think you would outsmart me at every turn." He did not appear at all indignant. Quite the opposite, his eyes were no longer that stark, cold silver, but were warm and brimming with mirth. "I'll go fetch my bags now. Grandmama, don't let her lock me out."

Cara followed him to the door and watched him stride down the street to the stables.

He disappeared from view a few houses down.

She stifled her disappointment and returned to his grandmother's side. "Perhaps I ought to have been a little nicer to him. Do you think he only plans to stay the night and take you back to London tomorrow? Without me, I suppose. He cannot abide me."

Duchess Anne patted her hand. "You are a breath of fresh air to him. I don't think he minded your impertinence at all. He needs to be challenged from time to time, not to be swooned and fussed over by those young ladies constantly throwing themselves in his path. He needs to marry a clever woman, not one with pudding for brains...or dull cheese."

"I'm sure there are very clever young ladies in London. Lady Yvonne is one, but not in a nice way. Do you think he will settle on her?"

"He won't, my dear. I can see by the look in his eyes that he won't."

Cara leaned against the sofa's back in relief. "I hope you are right. I would never wish unhappiness on him."

"My grandson is a clever boy. He will come around to finding the right girl for himself."

Cara bussed her cheek. "Do you realize I now have a duchess and a duke under my humble roof? And I have no decent supper prepared. Nibbling on day-old bread and leftover soup will not keep your grandson's muscles finely honed."

She laughed. "Ah, you noticed his muscles?"

"Of course. They are hard to overlook, are they not?" She felt heat rise in her cheeks, for she had been honest in her response, as she always was around the duchess. But this was the lady's grandson, so she really had to think before she blurted whatever was on her mind. "Are you feeling all right? Do you mind if I leave you with Mildred for a few moments while I run to the Three Lions Tavern and order heartier fare delivered for our supper?"

"Not at all. Go ahead and do what you must. I shall be fine right here with my tea and lemon cake."

"I won't be long. We can sit on the veranda and watch the sun set when I return. It's a perfect day, not a trace of rain in the air. And isn't the breeze refreshing?"

The duchess inhaled lightly. "There's something soft about the air in Moonstone Landing. It warms my bones and soothes my heart. But run along now, don't delay."

Cara grabbed her bonnet and took off for the village square where all the shops, inns, and businesses were to be found. All were in sight of the harbor and hardly a five-minute walk from her home.

Her Uncle Joseph was the tavern's proprietor, and he ran a fine establishment catering to the local residents. But he was also talking of expanding his premises now that outsiders were beginning to flock to their little patch of England's heaven.

Her uncle set aside the glasses he had been rinsing, dried his hands on a fresh cloth, and came around to hug her as she walked in. "Cara, love. How is the grand lady faring today?"

"Much better now that her grandson has arrived." She gave a wincing laugh. "I have both of them staying with me. I'm not certain for how long, but I should know more by tomorrow. In the meantime, can you have Wills deliver your finest meal as soon as possible? I have nothing decent to offer the duke."

Her Aunt Lettie bustled out of the tavern's kitchen in time to hear her request. "Only you would find yourself in such a fix, Cara. And here we were so worried about you when the squire's son abandoned you at the altar. But you seem to have gotten over the hurt. Won't he regret it when he hears you are entertaining a duke and a duchess?"

"We always knew those Covington boys were no good," her uncle muttered, referring to the sleepy village nestled in the cove to the west of their own. Her former betrothed had been born and raised there.

Cara sighed. "There is nothing wrong with the Covington boys."

"But one broke your heart only three years ago," Aunt Lettie reminded her.

"He did not. I broke it off," she said, knowing her words would go unheeded. "I was hardly more than a child. I had just turned seventeen and had not yet gained confidence in my decisions. I was swayed by others, as you well know since you were very much in favor of the match."

"You were recently orphaned, and we thought we were doing right by you," her uncle said with a shake of his head. "I'm truly sorry it ended badly."

"I know, Uncle Joseph. I do not blame anyone but myself. However, I would appreciate no one mentioning that unfortunate betrothal again. It is certainly none of the duke's business. He is already peeved I brought his grandmother here. I'm worried he will take her back to London at the slightest prompting. We do not need to give him a reason to take her away. Besides, as I said, Harlan did not end the betrothal. I did, and the timing of it was not well done of me."

Her aunt patted her shoulder. "Don't worry, love. We'll keep our mouths shut about that disaster. And if you feel better about saying it was you who ended the betrothal, then that is what we shall say, too."

Cara gave up.

After all these years, even she was starting to believe the gossip circulating about her unfortunate wedding day. Her parents had passed away the year before, and she had been too young to know what she was doing. Everyone in the family wanted her to accept Harlan's proposal, so she had. But standing in the church rectory, knowing there was no turning back once they entered the church and reached the altar, she'd taken Harlan aside. "I cannot go through with the ceremony."

He'd stormed out in anger.

Yes, it was terrible of her to back out on the morning of their wedding, but she could not find it in her heart to marry a man she did not love. He was happily married now to the right woman, a lovely Covington girl who had adored him all her life.

Which now left Cara at the age of twenty, unwed, and with no prospects of marrying any time soon. She did not mind, really. Being a spinster, which was her likely fate, was better than being unhappily wed.

After the mess she'd made of her betrothal to Harlan, no man in Covington or Moonstone Landing dared come near her. "I had better return to Duchess Anne. Do tell Wills to hurry. I'm sure the duke has built up an appetite after his long day's ride."

Speaking of the man, she saw him carrying bags from the stable, one slung over each broad shoulder and a third held in his hand. She hurried over to him. "I can help with the smaller one," she offered.

He shook his head. "No, it's heavy. I'll manage. Why are you not with my grandmother?"

"Mildred is looking after her, and I was only gone a few minutes to order food from the tavern for you. You do not look like the sort to eat like a sparrow, so I've had some heartier fare sent over. I'll shop tomorrow for more, once I know how long you'll be staying."

"That's easy. I'll be here as long as my grandmother stays."

Cara nibbled her lower lip in worry. "Will you allow her length of stay to be her decision? Or are you going to cart her off against her wishes?"

"Don't press me for answers, Cara. You will not like them. For now, let's leave it as I don't know."

"Fair enough." She sighed and hurried ahead of him to open her front gate and then her front door. "Your room shall be the large one on the right at the top of the stairs. It is where my parents slept. The bed ought to be comfortable, although I expect you are used to finer."

"You forget, I have been on the Continent most of these past few years. Home merely a few months between Napoleon's exile in Elba and his escape. Most of the time, my bed has been a patch of ground or a cot whenever I could find one."

"Oh, yes. I did not think...well, the sheets, blankets, and drying cloths are clean. I'll bring up fresh water and soap for you. Let me know if there is anything else you need."

"I'll be fine, Cara. You needn't fuss over me. Where's my grandmother?" he asked as they strode in to find the parlor empty.

"She must have returned to her room to pretty herself up for you. I'll look in on her next. Before I leave you, I would just like to thank you."

"For what?"

"For coming out here. You are the best medicine your grandmother could ever receive."

He eyed her with astonishment and something else in his gaze she did not quite understand. Goodness, this man simply devastated her senses. Perhaps Lady Yvonne felt this way about him, too.

Had she been too quick to judge the London beauty harshly?

What if Lady Yvonne did love the duke?

Well, he wasn't going to give her hastily tossed, ill-mannered opinions of the society diamond any credence.

But Cara quietly resolved to curb her tongue and be more careful in what she said.

She hurried to the kitchen to let Mildred know to expect her cousin with a large delivery. "Let me see to Duchess Anne, then I'll come back and help you set the table."

"Thank you, Miss Cara."

But Mildred looked perplexed.

"What's wrong?"

"You see, I had hoped to leave early tonight. My husband and I were married on this day twenty years ago. I thought…no, it doesn't matter. He will understand."

"Nonsense. I'm so sorry, I forgot. Of course, you must go home to him. Just help me put things in order and then go. I'll finish up the rest on my own tonight."

"But the duke—"

"Will just have to manage like the rest of us. It is fine. He'll have time to spend alone with his grandmother while I clean up. He won't notice a thing different."

"Thank you, Miss Cara." Mildred gave her a hug.

Cara went off to help Duchess Anne.

She knocked lightly at her partially open door. "How are you doing?"

"Quite well, my dear. Here, come help me with my earbobs. I think my hair needs a light brushing, too."

She took the brush, ran it gently through the duchess's thinning, gray strands, and pinned them up prettily. Then she helped put the teardrop pearls to the lobes of her ears. "Shall I fetch a shawl for you? The robin's egg blue, I think. It brings out the blue in your eyes."

The duchess laughed. "My dear, I am an old lady, and no man is going to be enticed by me whatever the color of my shawl. But blue it shall be because I think it is your favorite."

Cara shook her head. "What matters is what you like best. But it is perfect for this time of year. Shall we see if your grandson is ready and awaiting us in the parlor?"

"Yes, indeed."

It turned out he had washed up, changed his clothes, and was standing with his legs slightly apart and arms crossed over his chest while staring out a parlor window, his gaze on the sea.

"Nice view," he said, turning to face her as she escorted his grandmother to the sofa.

"Yes, it is." She smiled. "I love it. Just wait until sunset. You won't find anything so breathtaking in London. The sea begins to sparkle, as though diamonds have been tossed upon it. And the sky—"

"Duly noted, Cara. You can stop making your case for Moonstone Landing. I'll make my own decisions about the place. I don't need you carping about it."

"Carping?" Her smile faded and turned into a frown.

Had she started to soften toward him?

He was still an insufferable clot.

"I was merely making conversation. But I suppose there is no talking to you." She turned to his grandmother. "Will you excuse me a moment, Duchess Anne? I think I hear Wills coming up the walk with our supplies. I'll leave you in the care of your grandson while I put together our supper. You must forgive me, but I can only take him in small doses."

She felt his grin at her back as she started for the kitchen.

And heard his grandmother berating him, just as he deserved. But she thought no more about the man and hurried to the back door to greet her cousin. "Thank you, Wills. My, that smells delicious."

Her cousin was a strapping young man of sixteen with a mass of curly, brown hair and hazel eyes similar to the color of her own. His name was Arthur William Angel, but everyone called him Wills.

"Ma's an excellent cook, but she's also a snoop." He set down the basket of food and crossed the kitchen to peer into the hall. "I'm supposed to report back about the duke. What can I tell her?"

Cara laughed. "That he…" No, she had to curb her tongue, for whatever she said about him would spread through town like wildfire. "That he is a very good man. A brave soldier and loving grandson."

Well, it was all true.

"I hear he led several important campaigns against the French. Do you think he would talk to me about them?"

"I don't know. He might. Give it a few days and we'll see. Let him settle in before you accost him."

"All right." He kissed the top of her head. "Enjoy your meal. Keep out of trouble."

She frowned at her cousin. "I have no intention of getting into trouble."

"I'm just saying, Cara. You have a duke sleeping in your home."

She gave his arm a playful swat. "With his grandmother!"

He grinned back at her. "Don't be angry with me. I'm just trying to protect you. You know how rumors get blown out of proportion."

"Yes, unfortunately, I do."

Mildred joined them in the kitchen now that she'd set the dining room table. "Hullo, Wills. Are you headed back to the tavern? Give me a moment, and I'll walk with you. Miss Cara, I'll set the food on the platters, and then would you mind if I left with your cousin?"

"Not at all. I'll handle things from there," she said with more confidence than she felt. Her cousin's comments had disturbed her. Were rumors already starting? What was she to do about them?

The duke would not care, but she already had a matrimonial scandal behind her. One such misstep might be overlooked, but two? Perhaps if the duke were not so gorgeous…but he was.

She was so lost in her concerns, she did not immediately realize she had overlooked ordering something suitable for said gorgeous duke to drink. She and his grandmother usually had lemonade or cider with their meal.

But he would not be satisfied with such tame fare, nor would she blame him if he cast a remark about her oversight.

Her distress as the three of them were now alone and seated around the dining room table must have been obvious.

"Cara," he said, his voice a gentle rumble. "Is something wrong?"

"I am so stupid. I was at the tavern and completely forgot to order wine or ale or brandy for you. I'm so sorry. It was not done on purpose."

He surprised her by setting his hand lightly over hers. "It is fine. I'll have cider. We'll correct the oversight tomorrow. I'll stop by there and select for myself."

He eased his hand off hers and inhaled. "What is that? The aroma is spectacular."

Duchess Anne smiled. "Cara's aunt is an excellent cook. She and her uncle run the local tavern. I've put on a bit of weight since arriving here. Her game pie," she said, pointing to one set on a tray in the center of the dining table, "is exquisite."

They all dug in.

To Cara's relief, the meal proceeded smoothly. Perhaps it was because the duke was too busy eating to insult her further. Although he'd been quite nice about her neglect regarding the wine and ale. They even lingered over the meal, listening to him speak of those final days at Waterloo. "It was a close thing," he said in a respectful tone. "Had Blucher not arrived with his regiments, the outcome might have been quite different."

She and his grandmother were rapt.

"The Scots Greys distinguished themselves on the field of battle, a relief considering they hadn't seen much direct action during the war. But Scots are fighters, and their cavalry units came through for us. Lord Castlereagh decided to leave them behind to keep the peace in France until matters are more settled. But we have Napoleon back in custody, and he will not escape St. Helena's."

He spoke of others who had fought beside him, but Cara knew he had distinguished himself, as well. She found his modesty surprising, especially since he seemed to be arrogant in most things. The more he spoke, the harder she found it not to like him.

But he was so curt with her.

And yet, not when she had actually done something wrong. She still could not get over how forgiving he was about suitable drinks for himself. "Your Grace, you could have paid someone to fight in your stead. Why did you not come home after your grandfather died and you stepped into the title?"

He shrugged. "It is very hard to leave when those who have braved the battlefield at your side for years are still out there facing peril. I'm not sure I can explain it. I know my life would have been far more comfortable back in England, but I did not have the heart to leave behind these men who had become like brothers to me."

He poured a glass of cider for himself as their meal was finishing. "Now, I need answers from you. How did you come to be my grandmother's companion? You seem to have a comfortable home here. Why did you leave it for London?"

She contemplated hiding the truth from him, but even her aunt was resurrecting her broken betrothal. It would be a matter of a day or two before he heard the gossip which was too juicy to pass up.

Moonstone Landing was a quiet village, and her *faux pas* was the most exciting thing that had happened here in years.

He needed to learn the true story from her first. "I came to London because of a broken betrothal."

His eyes rounded in obvious surprise, those silver orbs suddenly intent on her. "What happened?"

She put a hand to her cheek as though this mere action would prevent her face from turning red with embarrassment. "My parents died when I was sixteen."

"I'm sorry."

She was surprised by how sincere he sounded.

Well, he wasn't a bad sort, just arrogant.

"Thank you. My Aunt Lettie and Uncle Joseph took over care of me. I inherited this house from my parents, but my aunt and uncle moved in here with me because I was too young to live by myself. It was only meant to be temporary…and it was, for they have their own apartment above the tavern. But the view is quite nice here, and it is a lovely cottage."

She shook her head. "But I digress. It wasn't long before a squire's son from the neighboring village took an interest in me. He was a very nice young man, and everyone encouraged me to marry him."

She glanced at the duke, waiting for him to say something.

He merely sipped his cider, his gaze fixed on her.

"I did not handle the matter of our betrothal very well. I accepted him, but almost immediately regretted it. I did not love him. Oh, I know most people scoff at the notion of love. But it was important to me. It still is."

"What did you do?"

"Everyone was so happy about the upcoming wedding, I could not find the strength to disappoint them. But as the day drew closer, this feeling of *wrongness* grew inside me. The morning the ceremony was to take place, I stood in the rectory and that feeling hit me again…like a roof collapsing atop my head. I could not walk through that door into the chapel. I told Harlan that I would not marry him."

"Let me guess," he said with a soft groan, "your Harlan did not take it well."

"Can you blame him? What I did was awful. I should have told him months earlier, but I could not muster the courage. He rode off in a temper, and no one saw him for days. The rumor then started that he had broken it off with me. I did not refute it. After all, what I did was cruel, and he deserved to be left with a little dignity."

She glanced at the duke but could not tell what he was thinking.

He took another sip. "How does he feel about you now?"

"Relieved we did not go through with the ceremony, I expect. He is happily married. But after that broken betrothal, my aunt and uncle decided I ought to go away to London for a little while. Another uncle of mine is a barrister there, and I stayed with him and his wife. That is how I met your grandmother."

Duchess Anne smiled at her. "We met in Hyde Park one day and got to chatting. We had such a lovely time, didn't we Cara?"

She nodded. "We started meeting daily after that, weather permitting. When I did not see your grandmother for several days, I grew concerned and called on her at her home in Ridley Square. I know it wasn't proper form at all, but those were beautiful days, and she should have been in the park. I was afraid she had fallen ill."

"Which I had," Duchess Anne interjected. "Cara asked what she could do for me. No one in the family had bothered to come around to see me or so much as send a note asking after my health. Cara's visit was just what I needed. Coincidentally, I had just received a letter from you, my dearest. So, I asked her to read it to me."

He frowned. "Really? A stranger? I might have written something sensitive."

Cara tried not to glower at him, but she was never much good at hiding her feelings. "I never would betray a confidence."

"Indeed, not," Duchess Anne intoned. "When you get to be my age, you develop a good sense of people. I knew Cara was trustworthy the moment I met her. When poor Dierdre could no longer serve as my companion, I asked Cara if she would consider the position."

"I readily accepted. I'd stayed long enough with my aunt and uncle and knew it was either return to Moonstone Landing or take on the role of companion to your grandmother. I was not ready to return home."

"We've had fun together, haven't we, Cara dear?"

She cast the elderly woman a smile. "Indeed, Your Grace. Every moment with you has been a pleasure."

The duke continued to regard her pensively. "I see. And my sisters did not like this blossoming friendship between the two of you."

His grandmother rolled her eyes. "They did not give a care about me in all the years you were away. It was only as I grew ill that they began to sniff around. They were determined to be rid of Cara, now viewing her as competition."

"For your affection?"

"They have no affection for me. That's the sad fact of it. They were worried I'd leave her my estate, what little of it is not tied up in trust. The thought had crossed my mind because your sisters really are quite odious in their greed. But Cara would not hear of it."

He glanced at her before returning his gaze to his grandmother. "Is that so?"

His grandmother frowned at him. "Yes, it is so. Cara has not asked a thing of me and never would. But your sisters did not believe my assurances. So, how better to be rid of her than accuse her of theft? That's how the nonsense about a stolen necklace came about, I'm sure."

He frowned. "I was home for several months between Napoleon's first exile and his final defeat at Waterloo. Why did I not see Cara then?"

"Are you suggesting I purposely fled from you? It was nothing of the sort. I had no idea you were returning to England, or I would have stayed and met you. I had to return home to take care of fixing up this cottage. My aunt and uncle had moved out, and they were urging me to sell it and invest the proceeds. I needed to see this place again and decide for myself."

"Obviously, you chose not to sell."

"I couldn't bring myself to sign the papers. Well, my Uncle Joseph is my guardian, and it would have been up to him to sign. But he loves me and would never go against my wishes. As I walked through this cottage, I had that same feeling again. That *wrongness* stopped me from taking the final step. Although this time, I hadn't taken it as far. No contract was signed. We never contacted a land agent, although several sought us out. I just knew the moment I walked through the door that I had to keep this place."

His grandmother nodded. "As I became weaker, we decided I should come here for the summer. It has done me good, Rowan. I have no wish to return to London yet. I'll let you know when the time is right."

"Grandmama…" he groaned.

"I know, my love. But it will all work out as it should." She reached her hand out to him. "Come, escort me onto the veranda, and we shall watch the sunset together."

"All right, sweetheart." He rose and helped his grandmother out of her seat. As he led her to one of the outdoor chairs, he realized Cara was not following them.

"I let Mildred go home early tonight." She cast him a wry smile. "So, I am left to clean up the remains of our supper."

He shook his head. "Leave it, Cara. I will help you afterward."

"You?"

He arched an eyebrow and grinned. "You look as though you are about to faint in shock. Dukes can do anything, don't you know?"

"Including wash dishes?" She stared at him in amazement. Honestly, this man had her completely puzzled. He was arrogant and curt over insignificant matters, yet kind and helpful when it counted. "Do you know how to wash a dish?"

"Why don't you try me and find out?"

Chapter Three

ROWAN STOOD ON the veranda, while the ladies took seats in time to watch the sun set over the water. He'd seen some beautiful sights in his life, and surprisingly, Moonstone Landing's scenic splendor was right up there among them.

He could see why his grandmother was thriving here, for the air was fresh and sweet. The tranquil sea, now bathed in sparkling golds and pinks from the sun's reflection on the water, had a way of soothing one's soul.

"Your Grace," Cara said softly, coming to stand beside him. "I'm going in to fetch Duchess Anne her sherry. Would you care for a glass?"

"No, I'm fine."

In truth, he was not fine. The years of battle had taken a toll on him, although he refused to admit it. But standing here, watching the day pass into evening and listening to the quiet rush of waves upon the sand beach, had him at peace for this brief moment.

He had forgotten what tranquility felt like.

He turned to watch Cara go into the cottage, his attention now fixed on the door, waiting for her to return.

"It is easy to like her, is it not?" his grandmother said, shaking him out of his musings.

He shook his head and laughed. "I have not reached a verdict on her yet. She's an odd girl. Never met anyone quite like her."

"Because she challenges you. She thinks for herself. And she does not prize wealth or titles over everything else."

He quirked an eyebrow. "That remains to be seen. Her friendship may be nothing but an elaborate ploy to steal your money. Or to get closer to me. Have you thought of that?"

His grandmother cast him a dismissive glance. "Yes, I am not dimwitted. Fortune hunters have been approaching me all my life. I have learned to tell who is genuine and who is motivated by greed. Cara and her family may not be *ton*, but neither are they paupers. They are happy with what they have and confident in who they are."

He leaned a shoulder against the railing post and turned pensive again. "Are you suggesting Cara is content to remain a middle-class spinster?"

"Honestly, Rowan. The girl is not yet twenty and one. Hardly on the shelf. What I am saying is that Cara is true to herself. She has opinions and values, and she will stand by them."

"If a duke offered to marry her, do you expect me to believe she would refuse him?"

"If she did not love this duke, then yes, she would refuse him. Are you referring to yourself?"

"Gad, no. It was just a hypothetical. I am trying to understand her and her motivations."

"Kindness is her only motivation. Oh, I hear her approaching, so I will speak quickly. She is a good soul and if you hurt her, I will never forgive you."

He was surprised by the vehemence of his grandmother's statement. Had Cara connived her way into the old woman's heart that deeply?

No wonder his sisters were concerned.

Cara walked out with a glass of sherry in hand a moment later. "Here you go, Duchess Anne. Isn't this sunset one of the prettiest we've ever seen?"

"Indeed, it is. But I fear my grandson's head is too filled with weighty matters to appreciate it."

"Weighty? I assume you are referring to his concerns over me." Cara turned to him and cast him a wry smile. "I am but a slip of a girl and not at all weighty, Your Grace. What you see of me is all there is. If you have questions, then ask them. You will get honest answers because I am a terrible liar. It is too cumbersome to keep all those untruths whirling in one's head, don't you think? I find it much easier to simply say what is on my mind. Would you care to know what I am thinking of you right now?"

He laughed. "No, you'll cut me to ribbons with that sharp tongue of yours."

"I'll try not to hurt your feelings. It is not in my nature to ever want to hurt others. All I ask is that you offer me the same respect. Simply because you view me as someone lesser than you does not give you the right to wound me with your glib words and accusations. I have a heart and it is fragile. Be honest with me but not cruel."

The girl had his head spinning again.

When had anyone ever spoken to him like this? Why was he made to feel like an oaf for wanting to protect his grandmother? "You want honesty?"

She nodded.

His expression turned serious, and he must have appeared quite daunting as he drew closer and folded his arms across his chest. "Then I'll tell you…"

Her eyes widened, and the little apple in her throat bobbed up and down as she stared back at him.

He leaned close and whispered in her ear. "I don't want to wash dishes."

She emitted a gasping laugh and shook her head mirthfully. "Serves me right. I've just talked myself out of an assistant. Well, it is more important for you to spend time with your grandmother anyway. I can manage the dishes on my own."

Having said that, she returned inside to attend to the chore.

"Rowan, really. You are too much. Are you going to let Cara do all the work herself?"

He grunted as he took the chair beside his grandmother and stretched his legs before him. "Of course not. I'll go in to help her in a little while. But she is quite capable of managing on her own, and I am not going to follow her in like a lost pup waiting for a pat on the head."

"Now you sound like a pouting, little boy."

"I am no longer a boy. I am fully a man, and it galls me that your Cara seems to best me at every turn. Perversely, I like her. But I am not letting down my guard around her until I am certain of her motives."

"Are you worried that my Miss Angel is no angel?" His grandmother took a sip of her sherry. "Rowan, there are good souls in this world, and she is one of them. I know most people who surround you want something from you. It is sensible of you to be wary. But don't close yourself off from the rare good ones because of it. Do you believe she is a thief? That she stole one of the Strathmore necklaces as your sisters accused?"

"No, I already know Joan and Ellen made up that story. I could see the lie in their eyes even as it spewed from their lips. You needn't worry on that score. But it does not mean I ought to trust Cara. She'll have to earn that from me."

"Fair enough, my boy." She took another sip of her sherry and returned her gaze to the sun setting over the distant waters. "Being here is good for my soul. I hope it heals yours, too."

He rose. "I'll go in to help her now. I won't be long."

He entered the house and took a quick look around the parlor. The room was quaint and well maintained. Walls painted a sunny yellow with crisp, white trim. Damask drapes and chair coverings in pale blue and dotted with yellow flowers. His bedchamber, while not the grandeur and elegance to which he was accustomed, was nonetheless comfortable and equally quaint.

He strode into the kitchen and saw her pouring hot water into a bucket. "Here, let me take over that chore."

She sighed in obvious relief. "Thank you. I'll clear off the dining room table meanwhile. Be right back."

He took a moment to glance around the kitchen, another well-maintained room which had a long table in the middle, a large hearth, sturdy ovens, an array of herbs hung on hooks overhead to sweeten the odor of the room, and copper pots that looked new.

He had just rolled up his sleeves when Cara reappeared carrying a fully laden tray. "I'll take that," he said with a frown. "I thought you were only bringing in a few glasses, not the entire supper. I would have helped."

She shook her head. "You are the oddest duke I have ever met."

"I'm likely the only duke you have ever met." He took the tray from her arms and set the load on the table. "It is bigger than you are."

"My spirit is tall and mighty." She glanced at his rolled-up sleeves. "I really did not think you meant to wash dishes."

"I told you I would. I am a man of my word."

She nodded. "I'll do the washing. Would you mind drying?"

"I'll wash. You dry." He tossed her a drying cloth.

"Truly odd," she muttered, shaking her head.

"And you are truly clever." He tossed his head back and laughed. "Not only do you have me washing them, but you have me insisting on doing so. Well done, Cara."

"You give me far too much credit," she said, her gaze fixed on his hands as he plunged them into the water and began to scrub the plates with efficiency. "I offered to do the washing, but you are such a contrary fellow, you have to do the opposite of whatever I suggest. So, it is your own fault. Admit it. If I were to say it is day, you would say it is night. If I claim it is warm, you would insist it is cold."

Curiously, a warm feeling curled in his stomach as he stood beside the impertinent girl, washing and then handing each plate over to her to dry. When else would he ever have been caught in a kitchen, cleaning up while a sharp-tongued girl berated him as they worked side by side?

The debutantes he had considered worthy of his notice had likely never stepped foot belowstairs in their homes. How many of them would have agreed to get their hands dirty to help him out?

He tried not to look at Cara, but it was hard to keep his gaze off her.

She was a beautiful girl.

Was she genuine?

He helped her put away the now clean trays, plates, and silverware, and did the same with the leftover food. They'd finished quickly while working together. "Thank you, Your Grace."

He nodded. "Let's rejoin my grandmother."

He was about to reach for her hand but stopped himself in time. Gad, the gesture had felt so right and natural. But he caught himself before he wrapped his fingers in hers and merely pointed toward the door instead. "After you, Cara."

That he'd wanted to take her hand horrified him.

Worse, why did he have the sudden urge to take her in his arms?

This is not how he expected to feel about the girl.

The sun was now low on the horizon as they returned to the veranda. "It is beautiful," she murmured, taking a moment to study the sky before turning to gently remove the now empty glass of sherry from his grandmother's hand.

Rowan pursed his lips in concern. "She's fallen asleep."

"She sometimes does." Cara secured the shawl around her shoulders. "It is nothing to be worried about."

"Should I carry her back to her bedchamber?"

"No, she'll wake up in a few minutes. Let her rest out here. Having you join us has made her very happy. I think all the excitement tired her out, but in a good way."

He laughed softly. "Are you being honest or merely polite?"

"Honest." She cast him a grin as she moved over to the railing and peered out toward the water. "I have no qualms about being impolite with you. In truth, you take it very well. I doubt there is another duke who would be so patient with me. Of course, I'd keep my mouth shut if it were someone else."

He joined her by the railing and leaned his shoulder against the post. "Why not with me?"

"Because...and don't you dare gasp in surprise...you are a good person."

"Why Miss Angel, seems you like me after all."

She chuckled. "Yes, I admit it. You are a fair and honest man, and you even have a sense of humor. Any other duke would have sacked me on the spot, but you indulged me. You took my jibes with a surprising lack of ill-temper. I think you like that I stood up to you. Few people ever dare, I expect."

He watched her as she spoke, studying the gentle curve of her lips and the shine in her expressive eyes. "In truth, no one ever does. However, impertinence can grow wearisome."

"Are you warning me to start behaving? You needn't. You know my feelings about your grandmother's situation. I've said whatever needed to be said. I hope going forward we can be civil to each other."

He laughed.

"Why are you laughing at me when I am trying to make amends?"

"I'm laughing at myself if you must know. I don't want us to be civil to each other."

Disappointment flashed in her eyes. "You don't?"

"I want us to be *honest* with each other. I want you to be who you are and not hold back your thoughts and opinions for fear of offending me."

The sparkle sprang back in her eyes as she regarded him. "No one has ever allowed me this…except for your grandmother, but she has a sweet heart, and I could never hurt her. And now you are being just as indulgent. Thank you."

It struck him then how vulnerable a heart this girl had.

He could so easily crush it if he weren't careful. "Cara, we may not always agree. But I never want you to be afraid to tell me what is on your mind."

"Truly?" She sighed in response to his nod. "You make it so difficult to dislike you."

He placed a hand over his heart in jest. "What? Did I just hear another compliment escape your lips?"

She shook her head and laughed. "Dear heaven, I hope not!"

He understood she'd responded in jest, for her eyes remained alight with mirth.

"Your grandmother assured me you were a good man, but I did not know what to expect. I think she is right. You inspire trust and confidence."

"I could not have earned the respect of the soldiers under my command otherwise."

She turned away to stare out over the water again. "You have done such important things with your life, valorous deeds. I cannot seem to do anything right. I hurt a good and decent man like Harlan. Now, you think I have abducted your grandmother and am trying to steal from her."

"I know you are no thief."

She gave a light snort. "You know I did not steal any necklace, but you are not yet certain about my friendship with your grandmother. Are you worried as your sisters are that I will steal their inheritance?"

"My grandmother has very little that is not already tied up in trusts."

She shook her head. "You needn't tell me what she has and what she hasn't. I don't care about any of it. But why would you believe me when I've done nothing to prove myself?"

He wanted to reach out and caress her cheek, brush back a stray curl of her lush hair as it blew gently in the wind, but quickly suppressed the urge. "My grandmother trusts you."

"She's a wonderful woman. I will feel such an emptiness in my heart when she is gone. Perhaps this is why I let her talk me into bringing her here. I needed her to see a little of me, of where I came from and where I'll probably live out my days. Her approval is important to me. And the lovely thing about your grandmother is that even if she does not approve, she has the kindest way of telling you so."

She cast him a sincerely warm smile. "I think she would have made an excellent army general. Like you, she has an inspiring confidence about her. Perhaps you inherited those qualities from her."

"Perhaps." He followed her gaze as she looked out across the water again. "She likes it here," he murmured. "I can see she is happy despite the constraints of her health. The sea air and sunshine have done her much good. And this view is spectacular."

"This is why I could not ever sell this place. Where shall I find anything so lovely again?"

"How is the water at this time of the year? Warm enough to swim?"

"Yes, Your Grace. Are you an able swimmer? It is generally calm, but one must always be on the lookout for riptides. Have you ever been caught in one?"

He shook his head. "No."

"They can be frightening. If ever you are, do not try to fight it. Just swim along with its current until you can break free. You will never win against the water. It is merciless and will claim even the strongest swimmers...as the former owner of Moonstone Cottage found out. Have you heard of it? It is quite the legend in this area of Cornwall. Look over there, it's the lovely house on the cliff overlook."

She pointed into the distance.

There were several stately homes visible on the rise, the finest one no doubt belonging to his friend, Cain St. Austell, the Duke of Malvern, and the one beside it no doubt the one Cara meant.

"The Killigrew sisters now own Moonstone Cottage, but it once belonged to Captain Brioc Arundel. He was a respected sea captain and a strong swimmer."

"I saw a commemorative marker with his name on it as I rode through town. Something about his dying valiantly while saving schoolchildren."

She nodded. "I was one of the children he saved. We were trapped on a sloop damaged and sinking during a sudden squall. As you can imagine, we were frightened out of our wits and huddled together knowing we were about to plunge to our watery graves."

"Cara..." He did not know what to say other than he was grateful she had been rescued. But that near-death experience must have impacted her deeply.

"He gave up his life to save ours." Tears clouded her eyes. "I still cannot think of that day without my heart breaking for his loss. From that moment on, I vowed to make something of myself as a way of honoring him."

She wiped a stray tear off her cheek. "But I haven't managed to do anything worthwhile yet. And that debacle over my betrothal to Harlan still weighs on me. I don't know how to make things right about that either."

"If your former beau is happily married as you mentioned earlier, then you have already made things right with him. He is with the woman who will give him a good life. As for everyone else, it is none of their business. I expect they keep that minor scandal alive because nothing else of interest has happened here since then."

"Until you came along and pounded on my door." But she was smiling at him, not in the least irritated with the highhanded manner of his arrival. "Now they will have this new scandal to occupy them."

"A duke at your door is hardly a scandal. Ah, I think my grandmother is stirring."

Cara hurried to her side. "Shall we go in now, Duchess Anne?"

"Yes, dear. Help me prepare for bed." She turned to her grandson. "I shall see you in the morning, my darling Rowan. I am so happy you are here."

He cast her a soft smile. "Take my arm, sweetheart. I'll help you to your bedchamber, then will leave the two of you alone to gossip about me."

He stood on one side of her and Cara on the other.

After helping her in and seeing her safely seated on her bed, he left the ladies. The night was still young, and he had no desire to retire yet. He returned to the veranda, fascinated by the sight of the moon rising over the water.

This place stirred one's soul even in the inky darkness of night.

He lost track of time as he caught himself up in philosophical thoughts about his existence and the reasons he had been led here. Was there a purpose to his meeting Cara? To being drawn away from the glitter of London ballrooms and elegant debutantes eager to gain his attention.

"There you are," Cara said, rejoining him. "Why are you standing alone in the dark?"

She had a lamp in her hand, for night had fallen quite rapidly. He had been too entranced with the sky's shifting display to bother seeking out so much as a candle for himself.

"Can't seem to draw my gaze away from the stars." But he did take a moment to glance at her. She looked so pretty by lamplight, her features soft despite its fiery glare.

She handed him the lamp. "This is for you. Stay out here as long as you like. I'll close up once you return inside."

"You needn't leave."

"I don't mind. You seem to be lost in your thoughts. I have no wish to intrude."

"You aren't. Stay out here a moment with me, Cara. Look how silver the moon is tonight. Is it always this beautiful?"

"Not always, but it is a perfect night. The sea is so still, like glass. See how the moon reflects upon the water." A moment later she raised her gaze heavenward to study a cluster of stars. "The skies are clearer than usual. Take advantage of this perfect view of the constellations. How pure and milky they look tonight. Are they not amazing? I must get around to purchasing a telescope for myself. I meant to do it last time I was home but got caught up in roof repairs instead."

"I would look up at those stars on nights after a battle, after the smoke had cleared and an eerie silence fell over the camp. The stench of battle never faded, but one could overlook it while taking in the sky. It gave me a brief moment of peace as we lay out there, unsheltered and exposed to the elements. Cold and illness claimed more lives than battle wounds, did you know?"

"The winters must have been brutal."

He nodded. "They were. For both sides."

She stepped closer to him so that their arms were almost touching. He wanted to close the distance between them, hold her tightly and bury his face against the gentle curve of her neck, inhale the lavender warmth of her skin.

But getting too close to this girl was the worst thing he could do.

First of all, he did not trust her motives yet.

Second, his grandmother adored her and would never forgive him if he took advantage of her innocence.

Third, she did something to his heart.

He wasn't certain what this feeling was yet.

But it was something he'd never experienced before. She had earlier described her feelings toward her former betrothed as *wrongness*. Did that mean there was a *rightness* to love? This is what he was feeling, a conviction that being with this girl was right for him.

Not that he was in love.

He wasn't.

He could not be.

But standing under the moonlight amid a brilliant display of stars, it was easy to think such a thing was possible.

Perhaps it was merely lust, a desire to kiss her and explore her body...to delve himself inside of her.

He shook out of the thought.

What he was feeling was something more than a mere lustful desire. He wanted to talk to her, listen to the lilt of her voice, and share his thoughts and ideas.

She was now going on about the stars and pointing out the various constellations. He listened because she was excited about them, and it gave him pleasure to learn about the things she felt were important to her.

After a few minutes, she paused. "Why did you let me babble?"

"I enjoyed what you were saying. Also, there's a gentle quality to your voice."

She laughed softly. "When I am not railing at you."

"Even that is music to my ears. I am so tired of being told whatever people think it is I wish to hear. Truth is always appreciated."

"Do not encourage me," she said, her grin wide, "for I will have far too much fun spouting my opinions."

They both fell silent, companionable ease developing between them.

Rowan took in the sounds of the night, the whistle of the wind off the water, and the soothing lap of waves upon the shore. Cara remarked on it a moment later. "The sound of the water will lull you into a deep sleep. If you leave your bedchamber windows open, you'll be able to hear its gentle whoosh upon the shore."

He grunted. "I haven't slept deeply in years. I can't seem to manage more than a few hours a night. Every little sound puts me on edge. It is what comes of too many years spent on a battlefield."

"Then you'll be up with the morning sunrise. It is also a spectacular sight. Well, I had better change into my bedclothes. Don't come upstairs until I return, all right?"

"I won't move a muscle. I can be a gentleman when I want to be. Have you ever slept on the beach, Cara?"

She nodded. "Once or twice with my father when I was a little girl. This is a perfect night for it. Are you considering doing this? Keep close to the stairs that lead down to it if you do. The tide comes in quite suddenly and will swallow up most of the beach and anything that happens to be on it. You had better spread your blanket by those stairs and nowhere near the water's edge, or you'll wake to find yourself buried under a wave."

"I'll keep to my bedchamber tonight and explore the beach in the morning. I think I'll take a morning swim, too. Or would you advise against it?"

"I think it is a wonderful idea. Just don't swim out too far, and test the pull of the tide when you first wade in. If it's too strong, do not be a fool and think you can win out. Remember those riptides. However, the weather has been quite mild these past few days, and our strip of beach is fairly sheltered."

She left his side to scamper upstairs and ready herself for bed.

The thought of her undressing in the room next to his put his head in a spin again. Would she need help unlacing her gown?

He could offer assistance.

Of course, he'd have his hands all over her body at the first opportunity. Even when restrained by her corset, he could tell her breasts were round and ample. He—

He needed to stop thinking of her.

He'd told her that he could be a gentleman when he wanted to be. Sadly, it seemed she brought out the sinner in him.

She returned while he was still fantasizing about her body…it was really not well done of him. Her hair was down and plaited in a loose braid that fell over one shoulder to rest upon one of her nicely rounded breasts.

Her robe was buttoned to her neck.

His hands itched to touch her, so he clasped them to the railing.

"Stay out here as long as you like, Your Grace. Just latch the door when you come back inside. I'll try to wait up for you to take care of it myself, but I may fall asleep before then."

"I'll take care of it, Cara."

"Well, goodnight then."

"Sweet dreams."

"And to you, Your Grace."

She left him and settled on the parlor sofa, curling up like a kitten.

He watched her through the open window.

Truly an odd girl.

Dangerous, too.

He could fall in love with a girl like her.

Chapter Four

CARA WAS NOT certain what to expect of the duke but had to admit she was pleasantly surprised by him. Almost three weeks had passed since his arrival, and they'd fallen into an idyllic routine. He did not sleep much, and she often heard him quietly moving about his bedchamber late into the night and again early in the morning, but the lack of sleep did not put him in ill-temper.

Quite the opposite, he seemed to smile more and was surprisingly undemanding.

He had gotten into the habit of stealing out of the house at sunrise each morning to take a swim. He always tried his best not to wake her, but the house was old and wooden boards creaked.

She would sneak out after him, not to ogle him as he undressed and dove into the water, but to make certain he did not get into trouble and drown.

But...oh, heavens.

The man had a finely sculpted body.

She never went down to the beach but remained crouched at the top of the stairs leading there to keep an eye out for his safety. However, this morning felt different. He was constantly glancing in her direction, as though sensing she—or someone—was watching him.

She sank back to hide against the hedges, not daring to creep back to the stairs until he had disrobed and was swimming in the water.

"I wonder how that feels," she murmured, wrapping her arms around her knees as she sat once more on the top step and watched him. She had never gone into the water again after the day she and her schoolmates had almost drowned in the storm.

But watching the duke cut gracefully through the waves, studying his powerful strokes, made her wonder what it would feel like to swim again.

Even the man's backside was beautifully formed.

It glistened like a pale, round apple amid the blue of the water.

She stifled a giggle, but really…was there any flaw in the man?

She shook out of the thought and returned her attention to the movement of his muscled arms amid the expanse of the sea. Her father had taught her to swim, but it had been so long ago.

Did one ever forget?

The duke suddenly waved to her as he waded out of the water.

She gasped, realizing he had caught her sitting on the step. But what audacity to show no shame as he strutted onto the sand in all his natural glory.

The cad even grinned at her and waved again, fortunately, this time after he'd donned his breeches.

Well, he knew he had an incredible body.

She could not have been the first woman to ogle him.

But it was not well done of her, and she did feel a little ashamed. Her insides warmed to a shocking degree whenever she caught sight of his taut, wet muscles.

She scrambled to her feet and hurried back toward the house.

He knew.

He'd caught her.

Well, it was bound to happen sometime. After all, she had been peeping for weeks.

She put a hand to her heart to stop its pounding and settled in one of the veranda chairs to await him. She caught sight of his magnificent form as he reached the top of the stairs and strode with confidence and not an ounce of embarrassment across the lawn toward her.

His shirt was open at the throat and droplets traced down his neck to disappear around his chest.

His dark mane of hair was damp and brushed back.

No wonder the wicked Lady Yvonne wanted him.

Who wouldn't?

He settled in the chair beside hers, his grin still broad and quite irritating. "Cara, you naughty thing. You have been spying on me. What happened today? You got careless and let me see you."

She cleared her throat, determined to brazen it out. "I wasn't spying…I was protecting you."

He chuckled. "And how were you doing that?"

"You went alone into the water. What if you had succumbed to a cramp? Or a shark had come into the cove to eat you?"

"Are you suggesting seeing me naked was a necessary evil?"

She tried to stifle a giggle, but it came out as a snort of laughter. "Yes, absolutely. You could have kept your breeches on if you knew I was watching you."

"And given you only half a show?" He shook his head. "Do I meet with your approval?"

Heavens, this man was beautiful.

"If I said yes, I would be stroking your conceit."

His gaze turned smoldering. "You may stroke me wherever you wish."

Her eyes rounded in surprise. "I ought to slap you for the remark."

"And I ought to spank you for peeking while I undressed."

"I told you, I only did it to protect you."

"Ah, that is a very good excuse. I shall have to use it sometime."

"Truly, I would not have bothered with you otherwise. But I was worried. Only fishermen are up at this hour, and they've already sailed off to fish. You would have been completely on your own and could have gotten into all sorts of trouble out there."

"And what could you have done about it?"

"Sounded the alarm. Woken my neighbors. Run into the water to help you."

He arched an eyebrow. "You would have jumped in to save me?"

"Yes, how could I not?"

His expression softened. "That is very brave of you."

She shrugged. "Just be careful when you are out there on your own."

The morning hinted of it being another hot day.

The sun was already beating down on the water. There was little dew remaining on the grass and no hint of a mist anywhere in sight despite the earliness of the hour. It would be another hour yet before Mildred arrived and prepared breakfast for them. "Would you care for coffee? I can—"

"No. Sit with me, Cara." He took her hand, entwining their fingers as he closed his eyes and emitted a sigh.

His hand was warm and comforting.

She ought to have drawn it away but could not find the heart to move.

He looked so much at peace in this moment.

She remained quietly beside him and gave thought to their plans for the day.

Duchess Anne had taken to rising earlier and often joined them at the breakfast table. This pleased the duke immensely. It delighted her as well, and although Duchess Anne tired easily, she was always eager for an outing.

They'd had a few days of rain this week.

However, on the sunnier days, she and the duke had gotten into the habit of taking his grandmother along the beach promenade or out for a bit of shopping in town. Afterward, they would stop by the local tea shop for Mrs. Halsey's excellent pies.

He would also find time to ride Ares for at least an hour each day, for his horse needed exercise. She wasn't certain where he rode the beast, but there were so many beautiful paths around town.

Today they had been invited to the home of the Killigrew sisters, Lady Phoebe and Lady Chloe, both of whom resided at Moonstone Cottage. They were young, Lady Phoebe barely seventeen and her sister perhaps thirteen. Their eldest sister, Lady Henley, was in London at the moment with the Duke of Malvern, who had insisted on helping her settle some family affairs.

Since her duke did not appear ready to release her hand anytime soon, she sat with him until she heard Mildred coming in the back way. "I had better go in."

He nodded and released her, his thoughts unreadable as he watched her. Indeed, she'd seen him glance at her pensively all week long when he thought she wasn't watching.

What was on his mind?

She resolved to ask him later, for there was much to do today, including preparing for their visit to the Killigrew sisters.

They arrived at Moonstone Cottage shortly after two o'clock in the afternoon.

"This is where your sea captain lived, Miss Angel," Lady Chloe said, greeting them as they entered the elegant home. This house, although referred to as a cottage, was more of a stately manor than a simple abode.

"Rumor has it this sea captain remained here to haunt the place after his death," Duchess Anne remarked. "Is that so?"

Chloe nodded. "He did, indeed. But he was on his best behavior after our aunt purchased the house from his estate. He fell in love with Aunt Henleigh and her with him."

Cara believed in such things and thought it was quite romantic, but she noticed the duke struggling to keep a straight face.

"How do you know he fell in love with your aunt?" he asked.

"He told us," Lady Chloe replied, casting him an impertinent stare.

The duke eyed her askance. "He told you?"

Lady Phoebe cleared her throat. "Yes, we all saw him. He really did haunt his home. We know he stayed on because of our aunt. She and our eldest sister share the same name, but they spell it differently. H-E-N-L-E-Y is the spelling of our sister's name. H-E-N-L-E-I-G-H is the way our aunt spelled hers. You appear dubious about our ghost, Your Grace. Do you not believe in love eternal?"

"Perhaps I shall become a believer when I fall in love."

Cara felt a flutter of disappointment.

It was foolish of her to care for this handsome man who was completely out of her reach. She and the duke may have forged a cordial working arrangement, but there would never be anything beyond it.

Her heart fluttered again when she saw him in conversation with Lady Phoebe.

They looked quite perfect together and were a match in rank. She was beautiful and a very nice person. All the Killigrew sisters were clever and charming, and despite being daughters of the late Earl of Stoke, a man much respected among the *ton*, they were not in the least haughty.

In truth, they were remarkably welcoming to all.

Lady Phoebe was the perfect hostess, and the afternoon passed enjoyably. Cara remained with Duchess Anne, while Phoebe and Chloe showed the duke around their home, pointing out the seafaring treasures held dear by Captain Arundel.

"We wanted to keep his memory alive because he'd done so much for the townspeople of Moonstone Landing," Lady Phoebe explained once they had rejoined her and the duchess in the parlor. "Miss Angel, you were on the boat that day. I cannot imagine the terror you must have felt."

Cara nodded. "I will never forget the captain's bravery. I used to swim in the cove often during the summer. But I haven't been in the water since that day. It still frightens me. Oh, I'll walk along the beach and collect shells. On occasion, I might dip a toe in the water."

She emitted a shaky breath and continued. "But to go in beyond that…I have never mustered the courage to do it. I suppose that makes me a bit of a coward."

Everyone was now looking at her with pity, even the duke who appeared surprisingly sincere in his concern. Why had she said anything about that day? Even now, merely thinking about it reduced her to tears. She quickly changed the topic of conversation. "When are you expecting your sister back? I hear she went to London. I'm sorry we missed her. Our paths must have crossed as we came out here."

"We hope she won't have to remain in London too long," Lady Phoebe said. "But the Duke of Malvern is with her, and he will look out for her."

"As he ought to do," Duchess Anne intoned, sparing a glance at her grandson. "Now that he is duke, he must be thinking of his duty, and I'm certain she'll make him a lovely wife."

Chloe giggled.

Phoebe grinned.

The duke coughed uncomfortably. "What makes you think he has any such intentions in mind?"

His grandmother cast him an impatient look. "Henley is a lady. He is escorting her to London. There is no question he intends to marry her, or he never would have offered to take her there. Obviously, he has chosen well."

He smiled wickedly at his grandmother. "Unlike me? Do not rush me. I know my duty well enough. Neither you nor Miss Angel were too keen on my original choice."

"That is true," Cara said, then snapped her mouth shut. It wasn't her place to give an opinion about his poor selection, certainly not in public. Who was she anyway to admonish him? Hadn't she made a mess of her own first choice? "I mean…ah, apple tart. My favorite. I think I shall stuff my mouth with it now."

The duke chuckled.

They left soon after because Duchess Anne was tiring, and Dr. Hewitt had planned to stop by later anyway. They'd taken a hired coach, and the driver was a cousin of her father's by the name of Mortimer Angel. When they returned to her cottage, the duke assisted his grandmother while Mortimer helped her down. "Cara, m'love. I see you are doing quite well. Stop in and visit us when you have a moment. The children are eager to see you again."

"I will Cousin Mortimer." She bussed his cheek.

"Let us know if you need anything."

She waved farewell and then hastened inside to assist the duchess. She also tried not to feel disheartened, for she had never felt the class distinction as strongly as she did today. It wasn't anyone's fault, certainly not Chloe or Phoebe who had shown her every kindness. But they were ladies, and it was obvious in the grace with which they moved and the charm with which they spoke.

On the other hand, she had an uncle who was a tavern keeper. A cousin who was a coach driver. Her father had been a solicitor, as was another of her uncles who had set up his office in London.

She had been well educated, but how could she possibly compete for a duke's attention against any of these elegant ladies?

No, she could not dwell on the impossible.

She caught up to the duke and his grandmother. "You look tired, Duchess Anne. I hope we did not overdo it."

"I had a lovely time. Help me undress, Cara dear. I think I shall have a light supper in bed. Ask Mildred to bring it in for me later."

"I'll let her know," the duke said and left them in his grandmother's bedchamber.

Cara helped her into her nightclothes and tucked the covers around her. "Are you sure you are all right?"

"Yes, dear. I am just perfect. As Dr. Hewitt will confirm when he stops by. Go look after my grandson. He'll get into mischief if he's left on his own for too long."

Cara laughed. "He knows how to behave himself. He's been surprisingly easy company these past few weeks. I never would have guessed it from our first meeting."

"He likes you. You are good for him."

Cara laughed again, certain the duchess was jesting. "Well, we haven't killed each other. That is an accomplishment."

"My dear, I am serious." She took Cara's hand. "Have you not noticed the way he looks at you?"

"As though he wants to throttle me? Yes, I've seen that expression a time or two."

"You are being purposely dense. He likes you, Cara."

She shook her head vehemently. "He tolerates me, Your Grace. That is something altogether different. Do you not think Lady Phoebe might be a match for him? It may be a year or two before she has her come-out, but your grandson would not mind waiting for her."

"And what of you? Do you not care for him?"

"Why should my feelings matter?" The heat of a blush crept up her cheeks. "I do like him, as you well know because you have a discerning eye. But it is ridiculous to think anything can ever come of it. Would he not be disgraced by marrying me?"

"Nonsense, child."

"It isn't nonsense, Your Grace. What put such a notion in your head? Are you not his grandmother? Do you not want what is best for him?"

"I do, my dear. Very much so." She gave her hand a gentle squeeze and stared at her pointedly. "I do. Open your heart, Cara."

Cara walked out numbly shaking her head.

Had she misinterpreted the duchess? Was she giving her approval of something beyond friendship between her and her grandson? It could not be.

The duke frowned as she approached him. He'd stepped out onto the veranda to watch the setting sun, as had become their nightly ritual. "Cara, what's wrong? Is she not feeling well?"

"She's fine."

"Then why do you look so...I don't know...confused? Perplexed?"

She put her hands on the railing and gazed out across the water, her attention caught by the blaze of reds and golds across the sky and the reflection of those brilliant colors upon the sea. "Just something your grandmother said to me just now."

"What did she say?"

She loved the sound of his voice, so deep and resonant.

It wrapped around her like a soft blanket.

Standing beside him made her realize how much she was missing by shutting herself off to love all these years.

Not that she loved the duke.

Of course, she did not.

It was absurd to think she could ever allow herself to do so.

She'd be utterly lost if she ever gave her heart free rein. He was the sort of man she could love deeply and eternally.

He would own her heart forever.

No, she could never free herself to love him.

His hands closed on her arms, and he turned her to face him. "Cara, what did she tell you? Why are you looking at me so oddly?"

"Truly, she is fine. She just asked to have her supper in bed."

"That's it?"

His face was so close to hers, she felt the warmth of his breath against her cheek. "No, she said something more. But it is absurd."

"Cara, I am going to throttle you if you do not tell me what is going on."

"Don't laugh. Promise not to laugh if I tell you."

"Laugh? Then it is not something serious?" He studied her face, his eyes upon her with a smoldering intensity.

"No, it is not serious. It is silly. Unthinkable. She said...she suggested...she thinks I am suitable for you. Is it not the most ridiculous thing you have ever heard?"

He inhaled sharply. "Are you serious? She said this?"

Cara nodded. "Ask her yourself."

"Not necessary. I believe you." His expression turned soft, and he cast her a smile. "Is this her way of telling me I should court you?"

"Oh, dear!" Her eyes popped wide. "Rest assured, I expect no such thing. I know it is impossible. That is why I suggested Lady Phoebe as a match for—"

"I have no interest in Lady Phoebe."

"Well, you've only just met her. But she is very nice, don't you think?"

He nodded. "For some lucky man. Not me."

She gasped. "You cannot still be thinking to take Lady Yvonne as your wife! Are you? I shall beat you senseless if you dare nod."

"Then I had better not nod," he said with amusement glittering in his eyes. "Why would it be impossible between you and me? Hypothetically speaking, of course."

"Isn't the answer obvious? I am not of good society. I am not of any society, actually. Marriage to me would make you a laughingstock among the *ton*."

"Do you think I care?"

She frowned at him. "You should care. These are your people."

"They are not. I don't know most of them and dislike the many I do."

"Now you are just making fun. You are a duke of the realm. You have a responsibility to king and country."

"How is marrying a frivolous, empty-headed peahen responsible? Do I not better serve my king and country by marrying someone sensible, compassionate, and kind?"

"Who is not of proper bloodstock?"

"Does your blood bleed red?"

She nodded.

"What an amazing coincidence, so does mine. We are of the same bloodstock. And why are you supporting this ridiculous Upper Crust nonsense when I should think an impertinent chit like you would heartily approve of bringing it down?"

"If you did not believe in the Upper Crust, then why choose Lady Yvonne as your likely bride?"

He sighed and released her. "Because I was not thinking straight when it came to marriage. I looked upon it as a business proposition and formulated a simple plan accordingly. Endear myself to a *ton* diamond. Marry her. Sire sons. Job done."

"That is the worst plan I have ever heard in my life."

"Ah, Cara. There you go kicking my arse again." He surprised her by caressing her cheek. "I agree. Thankfully, you stole off with my grandmother before I could put that miserable decision into effect."

"I do not mean to kick you. I'm certainly the last one who ought to berate your misguided wedding plans. At least you never proposed to Lady Yvonne. I left poor Harlan at the altar."

"And you've punished yourself by shutting yourself off from love ever since. Is it not time you forgave yourself?"

She could not deny it. "I want to fall in love," she said in a whisper, trying to hide the pain in her voice. "I think I am ready for it now."

"Then why not with me?" His hand was still lightly on her cheek, and he stroked across it with the rough pad of his thumb. "Why not me, Cara?"

Tingles shot up her spine. "Are we still speaking hypothetically?"

He nodded. "Yes, of course."

Foolish girl.

She had almost allowed her heart to believe the impossible could happen. "Then hypothetically, I would say a duke cannot seriously consider his grandmother's companion as marriage material. This means he would only be asking to take said companion on as his mistress, and that is something said companion would never do. Are we clear on this?"

He laughed. "Stop kicking me in the arse. I wasn't asking to make you my mistress."

"Good. Because I'll never agree to such a thing."

He dropped his hands to his sides. "I get it, you are a woman of good character."

She cast him a sheepish glance. "Not all that good. I spied on you naked."

He chuckled. "Ah, I forgot about that."

"Propriety is only part of the reason why I would never agree."

"What else is there?"

"Is it just you? Or are all men as dense?"

"Cara, you are kicking me again."

"As you deserve to be," she said with a frown. "We fairer sex have feelings which you constantly overlook. When a woman of good character gives herself to a man, it is because she loves him. Whether she comes to him as his wife or as his mistress, it is out of love. How do you think a mistress would feel when the man she loves goes off and marries someone else? Raises children with that other woman. Establishes a home with her. Conversely, how would the loving wife feel if her husband ignored her for another woman?"

"You are being naive, Cara. Smart women, whether wives or mistresses, manage to secure their futures. They negotiate the terms up front, whether it be with one man or a string of men."

"Love is not a negotiation."

"It is, Cara. No different than a business arrangement. It is a negotiation on whom to marry. Where to reside. How much to settle on the spouse and children. And for those men who choose to take on a mistress, it—"

She gasped.

"I am not saying I would be such a man. Indeed, I would not."

"Then why mention it?"

"Because I am speaking of men in general, not about myself. My point is that we negotiate everything in life. Love is no exception."

"That is where you are wrong. Love is a feeling that cannot be denied. When you love someone, you never have to worry about bargaining with them because love is about always supporting each other and protecting each other. Love is about giving, not taking."

"Cara, you are getting worked up."

"I cannot help it." She took a deep breath and continued. "Love is not about material wealth or possessions. It is about all the things that cannot be bought. Happiness, fulfillment, contentment, a meeting of the souls."

He raked a hand through his hair. "Gad, you make my head spin."

She cast him a wry smile. "Let me guess, that is not meant as a compliment."

She moved a few steps away from him because he was wildly attractive. She wanted to fall into his arms and succumb to his passionate kisses. No negotiation necessary. Was she that far gone in her affection for him that she would give up everything at his slightest encouragement? "I need to take a walk along the beach before supper."

"I'll come with you."

She was not pleased. "Don't you think we ought to give each other a little distance?"

"No. We are not done with this conversation." He took her by the hand and led her toward the beach stairs. He said not a word as they climbed down, their shoes clomping on the aged wood. When they reached the last step, she took a moment to slip off her shoes.

But she resisted when he took her hand again, because he seemed intent on leading her closer to the water. "Not there."

"You are afraid."

She nodded. "You know I am. I've made no secret of it."

"Yet you told me that you would run in to save me if I were drowning."

"I would." She nodded again. "And your point?"

His gaze searched hers. "Truly, Cara? Even though you are clearly afraid of the water?"

The sand felt warm beneath her feet, and a hot breeze swirled around them. "Yes."

"Scared as you are, you would jump in to save me?"

"Why are you so doubtful? My answer will always be yes because saving a life is more important than my fear. This is what Captain Arundel's valorous actions taught me. For years I wondered why I was spared. Do you not think of it yourself now that you have survived the war? Why are we still here when others are not? Is there some divine purpose to our existence?"

"And what have you concluded?"

She laughed wryly. "I have mostly questions and very few answers. But I know I cannot allow his sacrifice to be wasted. I think I was meant to live in order to save someone else's life—or at least make someone's life better. Well, this is what I have convinced myself of. I thought it might be your grandmother, but would it not be a grand jest if I was put on this earth for you?"

Apparently, he did not find it very funny.

"Me?" He stared at her quite seriously for a long moment, then shook his head. "My very own angel. How obvious? Why did I not see it before now? This is even your name, Miss Angel. Cara Angel...my dear angel."

"Are you mocking me?" She frowned at him. "All I am suggesting is that it is a possibility. Indeed, I could be completely wrong about all of it and will be of no use to anyone ever. As for my name, it is just coincidence. This village is full of my relatives who all go by the name of Angel."

"No, there's only one angel for me and that is you. I think I knew it the moment you slammed the door in my face when I first arrived."

"That is ridicu—"

"Hush, Cara. Even my grandmother sees that you are meant for me."

"But—"

He drew her up against him. "Close that pretty mouth of yours."

"Why?"

"Do you never stop arguing?" He hauled her into his arms and kissed her.

Chapter Five

ROWAN HAD WANTED to kiss Cara from the moment he set eyes on her but never planned to act upon that urge...until now. She was his angel.

She'd said it herself.

She was his Moonstone angel.

He was not going to let her go.

His lips captured her soft, giving mouth with passionate abandon, and he swallowed her up in his arms. She felt so right against him, her every curve fitting to him like the missing piece of a puzzle. The press of her lush breasts against his chest was utter perfection, as though she had been made just for him.

She even tasted sweet despite her acerbic tongue.

He wanted her, wanted to take her upon the warm sand and caress her in the same way the waves caressed the shore. He wanted to move inside her to the ebb and flow of the tide, pour himself inside her and make her his own.

He wanted to devour her, but also wanted something more.

He wanted Cara to love him.

He needed her love.

Needed her.

Lord help him, was it possible he had fallen in love with her?

He deepened the kiss and felt her respond with equal ardor because it was the only way she knew how to be, honest and willing to fully open her heart to him. He could have seduced her at this moment; he knew by the way she was clinging to him that she would not resist if he took the kiss further.

He was so tempted, for he wanted to watch her lovely face as she responded to the touch of his hands and the press of his mouth.

But he could not take her in this way.

He would never insult her by treating her as merely another conquest.

She wasn't that for him.

She was...

"Oh, dear heaven. What have you done to me?" She broke away and ran down the beach in tears.

"Cara!" Why could she not respond like every other woman he'd kissed? But no, she was going to turn him upside down. He caught up to her and grabbed her around the waist, trying to be gentle even as she fought to break away. "I am not going to hurt you."

"You already have," she said and kicked him.

"Now you've just hurt yourself." She was wearing no shoes and had likely bruised her toes against the thick leather of his boots.

He lifted her in his arms.

"Put me down!"

"No. You'll run away from me again, and I have no intention of letting you go. Do you hear me, Cara? You are my angel. *Mine.*"

"Put me down, you big oaf. Someone will see us and then my reputation will be in utter ruin."

"Stop struggling. You are never going to best me in strength. I will put you down, but first, you must promise not to run away." He liked the feel of her in his arms. He liked everything about this irritating girl. But she was such a contrary little baggage. Other ladies did not run from him after he kissed them. Quite the opposite, they always wanted more.

He never had to work hard to gain a bed partner.

Women flocked to him.

He did not even have to be actively on the hunt.

He was no coxcomb, but he knew he was handsome. Added to his wealth and title, no lady ever resisted him...except this beautiful bundle in his arms. "Promise me, Cara."

She grumbled but finally agreed. "I won't run."

"Good." He set her down and then crossed his arms over his chest and frowned at her. "It was just a kiss. A delightful kiss. Why are you so angry?"

"Because you had no right to kiss me."

"No, I don't suppose I did. But there is something between us, and we both feel it. Don't deny it. We feel it right here." He thumped on his chest at the spot over his heart.

"I don't know what you are talking about."

"Your problem is that you liked our kiss more than you expected, perhaps more than you could handle." He arched an eyebrow, awaiting her protest, but she looked ready to burst into tears again. "You gave me your heart the moment our lips touched," he said gently. "I know it, Cara. There's no use pretending it is not so."

She released a ragged breath. "I did not mean for it to happen."

"I know, but it did happen and cannot be undone. There is no going back for us, so why not move forward and see where this will lead us?"

"No. Whatever my feelings are, it will change nothing between us. I refuse to be your mistress." She tossed her chin up in defiance.

He could not resist giving that pert chin of hers a tweak. "Did I ask you to be? Is this all you think of me? I do not want that either."

She had been glowering at him, but now regarded him with some surprise. "You don't?"

"You look insulted. But I will not have you as a dalliance. I think you can be something more. Someone quite dear to me. However,

I've known you less than a month. I am not going to make you any promises."

He cupped her face in his hands, loving the delicacy of her features and the fire in her teary eyes. "What I am going to do is court you properly. I am going to court you as a lady ought to be courted because you are one in every sense of the word, and you deserve my respect and honor."

She closed her eyes and swallowed hard. "And what happens when summer is over, and you return to London? The weather is already turning cooler, you can feel it in the night air. Autumn will soon be upon us. Please, do not spout love declarations when we both know this supposed courtship can only end badly."

He rubbed his thumbs lightly along her cheeks to wipe away the tears still falling upon them. "Do you love me, Cara?"

"I will not answer that."

"Fine, don't. I have my answer anyway. Those big, lovely eyes of yours reveal everything. But it would give me pleasure to hear you say it. You are frowning at me again. That is no way to respond to a duke whose intentions are honorable. What flowers do you like? I'll have dozens of bouquets delivered to you every day."

She rolled her eyes. "Don't you dare. I will not have everyone in town remarking on it. Besides, I have no place to put more than one or two of them."

"Then I'll buy you jewelry."

She gasped. "I am going to kick you again. I will not accept expensive gifts from you. Is this how you think to court me?"

"How else is it done? I've never actually courted anyone before. Lady Yvonne is the closest I've come to it, and I was quite halfhearted about wooing her. She encouraged her suitors to inundate her with expensive gifts to win her favor."

"Because she is wicked and evil and cares nothing for who you really are. Don't give me *things* when all I want is you. Dukes really ought to be given lessons in proper courtship. It is for your own protection. Do you not see the difference between someone who asks only for your heart and someone who demands expensive gifts?"

"Of course, I do. But it is much easier to simply hand over *things* and not pieces of oneself." He laughed, knowing he was goading her. "You've clenched your hands as though determined to punch me."

Her expression softened. "I would never hurt you."

"I know. Nor will I ever hurt you. You must trust me, Cara." He did not take any of their conversation in jest. He loved her, but did he not need time to know it for certain? He was a duke, as she took pains to point out. She viewed his title as a wall between them and perhaps it was. The woman he chose to marry mattered not only to him but to all who worked his estates. His choice of wife would have far-reaching consequences, even on his standing in government.

But he did love her.

He had no doubt of it now that he'd kissed her and held her in his arms. Fire still flowed through him, and all he'd done was give her a kiss, a fairly chaste one at that.

He studied her as she was now studying him.

Marriage to Cara would never be dull or predictable. Not that he expected every day with her to be filled with chaos; he knew it would not be. It would be filled with love and happy moments. She would challenge him to be a better person, to make a difference in the lives of others just as his leadership had made a difference on the battlefield.

Since Cara did not hold back her feelings, he knew their coupling would be as passionate as her surrender to his first kiss. "Dry your eyes, Cara. We'll talk more about this tomorrow."

He took her hand and led her back to the steps where she'd left her shoes. "Are you certain you don't want a diamond necklace?"

"Like the one I supposedly stole? I am going to kick you again."

"Blast, I forgot about that completely. You know I did not mean it that way. I find it quite ironic that the one girl I would like to bathe in gemstones will have none of them. What good is my wealth if I cannot show it off to you?"

"Your arrogance is proof enough of the extent of your fortune." She cast him an impudent smile, which eased his mind because he did not want her to be upset with him. They were both surprised and off stride over their feelings for each other, but that was something they could work out over time.

He gave a mock wince. "Ouch, you are kicking my arse again. Well, you let me know if you have a change of heart. My pockets are always open to you."

She sank onto the bottom step and wiped the sand off her feet. "I won't. Are you purposely trying to annoy me? I want your love, not your bank account."

He wanted to kiss her again.

Was there ever a more perfect girl created for him?

Of course, his grandmother had known it probably from the first moment she met Cara.

He knelt beside her to assist her in donning her shoes. "How about apple tarts? Would a gift of those be more acceptable?"

She cast him another impudent smile, mirth shining in her eyes. "I can be bribed with those. But don't you dare buy out the shop. Then everyone in town will be angry with both of us. One or two will be quite satisfactory."

Lord, how was it possible he'd fallen so hard and fast for her?

But how could he not?

Cara truly was someone special.

And she had a gloriously kissable mouth; he'd thought so from the first. "Look at me, I am already on bended knee before you, Cara. Perhaps I ought to propose just to get it—"

"Don't you dare!" She pushed him onto the sand and bounded up the steps.

Chapter Six

ROWAN WORRIED THAT he would awake and realize yesterday had been a mistake, but he knew it wasn't the moment he crept downstairs and caught a glimpse of Cara curled up in a little ball on the sofa.

He paused a moment to watch her sleep, but he did not wish to disturb her. He was on his way out for his early morning swim and would seek her out when he returned.

She was an angel.

If anything, his heart had absorbed her even more deeply overnight.

It was an odd feeling to have not a doubt about something as important as marriage.

"Good morning, angel," he said in a whisper and brushed a light kiss on her forehead before heading down to the beach.

The sun was already beating down on the grass, and it promised to be another hot day. He hurried down the steps, disrobed on the sand, and then dove into the sparkling blue water. The water was cooler than the air surrounding him and quite bracing.

He had almost finished his swim when he noticed several fins gliding in the water toward him.

Oh, hell.

Sharks?

He was too far from shore to reach it safely if those fish intended to make him their breakfast. But as one of those sleek, gray creatures lifted out of the water, Rowan let out a breath in relief.

They were dolphins.

Those creatures were known to be friendly, weren't they? But as they now surrounded him, he was not certain of their intent.

One swam past him, splashing water onto his face with its powerful tail. It turned and swam back to gently poke him with its snub nose. "Ah, you want to play. Is that it?"

When another swam by him, he grabbed onto its fin and allowed the creature to carry him along for a ride. But he had no intention of hanging on beyond the confines of this protected cove.

To his surprise, the dolphins seemed to understand this and merely took him in a circle around the cove. He was having so much fun, he paid little attention to the time passing until he heard someone shouting to him.

He looked toward the stairs and saw Cara rushing down with a stick in hand. Lord, did she think he was in trouble?

Was she going to jump in to save him?

Of course, she was.

This was Cara, a fierce little thing and so full of heart and courage.

He let go of the dolphin's fin and swam hard toward the shore. But they must have thought he was still playing and continued to swim beside him, cutting in front of him and nudging him from time to time.

He saw Cara lift up her nightgown to her thighs and wade in, his very own angel come to rescue him. "It's all right! I am not in danger!"

The wind blew his words toward the open sea.

He reached her as she had the stick upraised and was preparing to strike the biggest dolphin on the nose.

Rowan grabbed the weapon out of her hand and tossed it back onto the sand.

"What are you doing?"

"I don't need saving," he said with a laugh, scooping her up in his arms.

Hell.

He was naked.

He could not carry her out of the water as he was, so he stayed where the water was up to his waist. "Did you see me, Cara?" He could not contain his smile. "I swam with the dolphins. It was amazing!"

She looked about warily as those gray giants glided close.

"They're friendly. I promise. See?" he said when one came up and gently touched her toes with the tip of his nose.

She shrieked in delight.

He planted a kiss on her lips. "Lord, you are the prettiest fish I have ever caught."

"I mistook you for a duke, but I see you are Neptune, god of the sea." Her smile was broad and sparkling, and the moment was something likely never to be repeated. The sun shone down on them while his new friends, the dolphins, playfully leapt in and out of the water behind them.

Most of all, Rowan had Cara in his arms, and she was soft and beautiful.

"Well, this god has no clothes on, so you had better close your eyes while I carry you out."

She wrapped her arms around his neck. "You looked wonderful out there. But I was afraid they were going to run off with you or suddenly turn on you and eat you."

He kissed her on the lips again, certain she tasted sweeter with every kiss. "I was never in any danger, not with my angel to protect me."

He slogged out of the water, set her down on the sand, and took her by the shoulders to turn her away. "Close your eyes and don't peek."

"I've already seen you naked."

"I know, but never up this close. And I am already responding to your nearness."

"What do you mean?"

He laughed. "I am not going to tell you. But I will show you at the proper time. Come on, let's go back to the cottage before I do something untoward. Your body is too luscious to ignore."

He hastily donned his trousers and shirt, then raked fingers through his wet hair to brush it back. He bent and scooped up his boots, merely carrying them in his hand as he and Cara started up the steps.

She glanced at him as they strode together. "You have a huge smile on your face."

He nodded. "I've never been happier. Seriously, Cara. All of it, the cottage, the beach, the sun and sand, the dolphins. Most of all, you. I never thought to experience such contentment."

She returned his smile. "I know what you mean. It's this place, Moonstone Landing. One can forget the cares of life here."

"But life still goes on around you. This village isn't some hidden place reached only by casting a magical spell."

"I'm afraid it will start changing soon. Already the inn is expanding to accommodate more visitors. My uncle is about to do the same with his tavern. The Duke of Malvern has taken up residence here…at least, for now. The Killigrew sisters have done the same. We are attracting London society. Hopefully, we will change them for the better instead of having them change us for the worse."

He was holding Cara's hand as they approached her cottage, but he stopped suddenly and drew her behind him, for there were two unsavory-looking men standing by the door and about to knock on it. "May I help you, gentlemen?"

He used the word loosely.

"We are here for Miss Cara Angel. She is to return to London with us," one of them said, withdrawing an official-looking parchment and handing it to him. "Ye can see it is a warrant signed by Lord Fortesque. And who might ye be, sir?"

"The Duke of Strathmore, and you shall address me as Your Grace. What nonsense is this? Is my grandmother aware of this? Why has such an order been issued?"

He kept hold of Cara's hand as he scanned the paper. He could feel her trembling as she pressed against his body, for she fully understood the gravity of the situation. Those men were already eyeing her and would give chase the moment she attempted to run inside.

He was not letting go of her.

Nor would he ever allow these men to take her.

"I understand she is the companion to the Duchess of Strathmore," one of the men said, "but that cannot protect her. She stole a necklace."

"Whose necklace? And who reported it stolen?" He tried to keep his voice steady as rage tore through him.

"Why, I believe it was one of yer own heirloom pieces, Your Grace. Yer sisters reported it and filed charges against the thief," the second man said.

He was going to squash those two malicious wasps the moment he returned to London. "What gives them the right to act on my behalf?"

"Ah, Your Grace. It is not our place to question the specifics, but Miss Angel was seen taking the necklace in question by one of their friends...a Lady Yvonne—"

"It is utter nonsense! I shall have Lord Fortesque's head on a pike if he does not rescind this warrant immediately. In fact, I shall do it for him." He tore the parchment to shreds. "No one touches Miss Angel, do you understand me?"

The men did not take too kindly to his pronouncement.

"Is this the lady in question?" the first one, a big man with an ugly countenance, asked as his gaze fixed on Cara. "I'm sorry, Your Grace. But we must take her in."

Rowan blocked them when they tried to reach around him to grab her. "You will not touch her!" he said with a roar. "This is my wife. She is no longer Cara Angel but the Duchess of Strathmore. Even you know that a duchess cannot be put under arrest. Such an order can only come from the Crown, not a common judge such as Lord Fortesque. Begone before I have you hanged for assaulting a duchess. Do you understand me?"

They backed away but did not leave.

The second man, equally large and with a scarred face fierce enough to scare small children, held out his hands in supplication. "Then the matter is easily settled by showing us proof of the marriage. Your Grace, that is all we need, and we shall leave without causing ye any more grief."

"You need no more proof than my statement uttered here and now. I am the Duke of Strathmore, and I have taken Cara Angel as my wife."

He stepped on the torn shreds of the warrant, sorry he was not wearing his boots to better grind them into the ground. With a firm hold on Cara's hand, he stormed into the cottage and latched the door securely behind them.

"Blessed saints, are you all right?" He hugged Cara fiercely to him. "I am never going to let them touch you."

She looked up at him, her face ashen. "How can we avoid it? They have a signed warrant in hand."

"*Had* a signed warrant."

"Your ripping it to shreds does not change its existence."

He glanced toward the kitchen. "Go see if Mildred is here yet."

"Why? I don't want her to get in trouble for—"

"Have her run to your Uncle Joseph and tell him to meet us at the church right away."

"The church? To have the minister give me sanctuary until this matter is worked out? What makes you think these men have any respect for the church? What if they burst in and grab me?" She took a deep breath and peeked out the window. "They don't appear to be pious. But they do look restless. Do you think they will break down the door?"

"They won't dare. Not while I am standing here to guard it. And just to be clear, my plan is not about providing sanctuary for you. I intend to marry you, but I need your uncle's consent since he is your guardian."

She gasped. "Are you mad?"

"Do you want to marry me or not?"

"I dream of it every night, but—"

"Good. Matter resolved. Ah, Mildred," he said, silently blessing the woman for her promptness as she entered through the back door and scurried into the parlor to see what all the commotion was about.

Rowan quickly explained to her what needed to be done.

"At once, Your Grace." She hurried off out the back way.

He arched an eyebrow and chided Cara, who still seemed troubled by his idea. Not for herself, but she obviously felt as though she was trapping him into marriage. "You see, she does not waste precious time by asking a thousand questions. Go wake my grandmother. Although how she could still be asleep with all the excitement is beyond me. But I suppose age slows one down."

"My hearing is still perfect," Duchess Anne intoned, leaning on her cane as she made her way into the parlor.

Cara ran to her to assist her into a chair.

"My dear, why are you trembling?"

"Those men outside want to take me back to London," she said, her voice still shaky. "Your granddaughters have filed charges against me for stealing a family necklace, and Lord Fortesque issued a warrant for my arrest."

"Those horrid creatures! Rowan, what can we do?"

"I am going to marry Cara. It is the only way to protect her. I just—"

"It is the only immediate way to protect me," Cara interjected. "But I'm sure the odious warrant will be rescinded when your grandson explains the mistake. After all, he is the duke, and it is a Strathmore necklace. If he refuses to bring charges, the matter will be dropped."

"It could take weeks to untangle. You are not spending a moment in the custody of those men." He turned to his grandmother. "I have to get her to the church before they figure out I've lied to them."

"What did you tell them?"

"That we are married already, and she is my duchess." He turned back to face Cara. "I do not want to hear a word of protest out of you. Those witches are my sisters. It is my duty to make things right. Stop frowning at me. Are you not scared out of your wits?"

"Yes," she admitted.

"And do you not love me?"

She frowned. "But what about you? They are the ones who wronged me, not you. Why should you be the one to suffer the punishment?"

"Cara, do you love me?"

"Yes, I do. How can any woman resist you? You are magnificent in every way, as you well know. However, you can be irritatingly arrogant. But the dolphins adore you, and animals have a very good sense about such things."

He grinned. "More than I needed to know but thank you."

His grandmother was chuckling as well. "Rowan, she is still fretting. You must tell her."

"Tell me what?" Cara seemed genuinely confused, but Rowan understood what his grandmother was asking of him.

"That I love you," he said, still peering out the window to make certain those men were not concocting a plot to snatch her. "This is not how I ever intended to tell you, certainly not with my grandmother planted between us and listening in on my every word. I would punctuate my declaration with kisses, but I dare not take my eyes off those scoundrels for a moment. My kissing you will have to wait."

"You don't have to—"

"What? I don't have to kiss you? Or tell you that I love you? But I do love you, Cara. With all my heart. The only thing I hadn't planned on was the speed with which we must marry. That will cause another scandal, but one I'm sure will be overcome rather quickly. People forgive dukes and duchesses anything, as you will soon find out."

"How can you jest at a time like this?"

"It is no jest. You know the titled have privileges that commoners do not, which is entirely my purpose in marrying you within the hour. As for my feelings for you, I am not in jest. My interfering grandmother will assure you, I was lost to you the moment I set eyes on you. Now she'll take all the credit for making this happy match. She will be quite insufferable as she boasts about it to everyone."

He noticed the men now walking away, but he'd heard them say something about a constable and realized they were leaving to fetch the local official responsible for keeping law in the village.

He chuckled. "They've gone off to fetch your father's cousin, Malcolm Angel."

Cara looked up at him. "The constable?"

"Run upstairs and get dressed. Something suitable for a bride to wear. I'll toss on some decent clothes as well. Grandmama…"

"I'll only slow you down. Leave me here to delay those wretched men if they come back. You've made me so happy, Rowan. I knew Cara was perfect for you."

Cara kissed her on the cheek. "If anyone is an angel, it is you." She hurried off to get herself ready.

Rowan sighed and sank into the chair beside his grandmother.

"How did my sisters turn out so miserably? I'm going to put Bow Street runners to the task of investigating every London jeweler who is known to be shady. I don't even know which one of the heirloom necklaces they claim was stolen. But so help me, if one of them has pawned a single gemstone off it, I shall have them clapped in irons."

He leaned forward and buried his face in his hands. "Gad, to think I ever considered courting Lady Yvonne. She lied for them. She thought nothing of destroying an innocent. Thank goodness you had me chasing you to Moonstone Landing. Those three vultures would have eaten Cara alive if you had stayed in London."

"I know, dear boy. But they might still manage it if you do not marry her before those horrible men return." She patted his shoulder. "You needn't dawdle with me. Make yourself presentable, so Cara can truly swoon over you," she teased.

He sat up and laughed. "Thank you for bringing her to Moonstone Landing. I see now it was the only way to get me to notice her. I might have foolishly betrothed myself to Lady Yvonne if I had remained in London."

"I was ever hopeful you would see through that false diamond in time. But getting you away from her was not my only reason for wanting to come here. I am still quite ill, Rowan," she said quietly. "That part is no ruse."

"I know, Grandmama. Cara and I will take care of you. I hope you know that."

"I do."

He kissed her. "I love you."

He took the stairs two at a time and hastily dressed for his wedding.

When Cara was ready, he took her out the back way, and they ran to the only church in the tiny village. The minister was standing in wait for them, along with several members of Cara's family. But Rowan was only interested in her Uncle Joseph, for he was the one who had the authority to consent to their wedding.

The man was clearly the practical sort and did not waste time with needless negotiation. "I know you'll take care of our Cara," he said and quickly signed off on the license.

He and Cara exchanged vows moments later before the altar.

Although everything was rushed and a little confused, Rowan had no doubt he had made the right choice. He did not hesitate when it came time to recite his vows to love, honor, and protect the angel beside him. She did the same, her love for him shining in her eyes. But she was obviously still concerned about having pushed him to a hasty marriage.

Well, he'd remove all doubt in her mind tonight.

"How does it feel to be the Duchess of Strathmore?" he asked once the wedding ceremony was over, and the cheers of her family and other onlookers had died down. It was amazing how quickly word spread within the village.

"Too soon to tell yet," she replied with an impish grin. "But I think I am going to love being married to a handsome duke."

When even the Killigrew sisters, Phoebe and Chloe, rushed into the church to offer their congratulations, Rowan realized the two warrant officers might be the only ones in Moonstone Landing who remained unaware of the ceremony just taken place.

"Your Grace," Cara said quietly, "I don't know how I shall ever thank you for this."

"Protecting you is what matters most to me. You are my wife now, Cara. You need only refer to me as Strathmore when in company. But do you think you can call me Rowan whenever we are speaking privately? Or any other manner of endearment will do."

She cast him a radiant smile. "I would love to…Rowan. It feels so odd to call you that, but quite lovely. I fear to wake up from this splendid dream."

He wanted to take her into his arms and kiss her, but their moment aside from the crowd of well-wishers was over. They were about to be surrounded again. "I will always keep you safe."

"And I will always do the same for you."

"I know. This is why I married you. I was in desperate need of an angel."

Chapter Seven

C ARA WAS CERTAIN the day had passed in a dream, and she would wake up to find herself tumbled off the parlor sofa and nursing a lump the size of a goose egg on her head. How else could she explain the revelry that had taken place throughout the day?

Rowan had insisted on tossing a celebration and inviting the entire town. "I won't deprive you of a wedding breakfast."

But what he'd loosely termed a wedding breakfast turned into an all-day affair hosted by them, the Duke of Strathmore and his new duchess. The locals poured in from everywhere, and the kitchens of her uncle's tavern and the Kestrel Inn were churning out game fowl, fish, haunches of pork, meat pies, racks of lamb, and other hearty dishes throughout the day. Mrs. Halsey's tea shop was stripped of all her baked goods.

Somehow, musicians appeared, so there was dancing to be had, as well.

As day turned into night, being married began to feel quite real to Cara. "This is surely the loveliest wedding ever held. Even those sour-faced warrant officers had a good time. I'm glad they held no grudge for your outsmarting them."

"Plentiful food and ale will put a smile on any man. Despite their unpleasant countenances, I don't think either of them wanted to see you tossed in prison."

Cara had just tucked his grandmother into bed. Rejoining him now, she was eager for their time alone. "She is settled in her chamber, and I am sure the day completely exhausted her. She's probably asleep already."

Rowan took her hand and led her upstairs to the bedchamber he had been using as his own. The lone candle held in his other hand cast its soft light upon his finely sculpted features.

His lips twitched at the corners in the hint of a smile, and his eyes, the gray of smoldering ashes, held a rakish glint. "Much as I adore her, my mind is not on my grandmother tonight. I am trying to forget she is directly below us."

Cara stifled a giggle. "We could not have moved her to the inn, it would have been too much of a strain for her. Nor could we have left her alone here."

They could have asked one of her relatives to watch her, but neither of them had thought of it at the time. Everything had been so rushed.

He nodded. "Let's just hope she does not hear every noise we make."

"I will be as quiet as a mouse," she assured him, eager for the taste of his lips and the heat of his body against hers.

He laughed softly. "Cara, I surely hope not. I will have failed miserably as a husband if I do not have you howling my name when I properly make you my wife."

She thought he was jesting, but his wicked grin revealed he was quite serious.

Warmth flooded through her body.

Well, she was not completely ignorant of what took place in the bedchamber. Not that she'd ever had any experience herself. But this was the countryside, and she'd seen the local animals in mating season.

She had also gotten an eyeful of Rowan when he took his morning swim.

Heavens, the man stirred her most wanton thoughts.

Now that she was his wife, she would have free rein to run her hands along his magnificent body and explore it quite thoroughly.

He closed the door after them once they entered his chamber and set the candle on the night table beside the bed they would now share. "I love you, Cara."

He drew her into his arms.

She closed her eyes as a ripple of delight ran through her. "I love you, too. I'm so sorry our—"

"Don't apologize to me for any of what happened. It was mostly my fault. Those sisters of mine are malicious beyond belief, and I will see to them and Lady Yvonne shortly. But tonight is for us alone, for the promise of what our marriage will bring."

"It will be a beautiful marriage, I know it will."

They spoke no more as he began to undress her, his hands unfastening her ties with surprising ease. But she supposed he was adept with such matters from experience.

Her inexperience extended to matters beyond the bed. She never expected to be a duchess and had no idea what it entailed.

Questions whirled in her mind as he caressed her shoulders and rained soft kisses on each spot of skin he bared. She closed her eyes to absorb his touch, loving the feel of his hands and lips and looking forward to the intimate promise of this night.

But she knew the nobility lived differently from commoners.

Would she always share his bed?

She wanted their marriage to be true in every sense.

"Cara," he said gently, pausing as he was about to remove her shift. He had already removed the rest of her clothing and unpinned her hair so that it fell in a cascade down her back. "Here I am trying to seduce you, and your thoughts are elsewhere. I must be losing my touch."

He'd said the last in good humor, so she knew he was jesting.

Even though her mind was awhirl, her body was quite aware of him and already responding.

"What is on your mind, love?"

"Will this...us together...will it only be for tonight?"

His eyes darkened. "Do you want it to be?"

"No, I would like us to be in each other's arms every night if you will permit it. One bed for us, no separate quarters. But I've seen grand houses and know this is not how it is done. Dukes and duchesses each have their own quarters. Often, they lead separate lives. Everything was so hurried this morning, we had no time to sort any of this out."

She pointed to the bed her parents had shared all of their married lives. "This is what I would like. Us together."

He seemed to ease. "Then this is what it shall be. It is what I hoped for as well. Cara, I may look like a rogue, but at heart, I am not. I did not think it possible to find one woman to love and with whom I would grow old. But this is what I've always wanted. I am much like my grandfather in this way. You should have seen him around my grandmother. No matter the time of day or how horrid the weather, it was as though the sun always shone when she was beside him."

She drew in a breath. "Do you think we could have this?"

"Yes, love. I already feel this way about you."

"Truly?"

"From the moment I set eyes on you." He cast her a rakish grin. "Do you think we can get to the fun part now?"

She smiled as she helped him off with his shirt and gave a little squeal when he lifted her into his arms and set her on the bed. He quickly removed all but his breeches, then eased the shift off her body and settled over her. "You're so beautiful, Cara. I knew you would be."

He spoke no more as he went about the business of properly making her his wife. As for herself, she did not know what she was supposed to do but quickly realized allowing him to see her pleasure, to set herself free to respond to his touch, was all he was asking of her.

She liked that her pleasure also heightened his.

In truth, she could not contain it anyway. The touch of his lips and the stroke of his fingers, the flick of his tongue in her most intimate places soon had her in a fiery state of mindlessness.

She tried to be quiet, but moans escaped her lips so that he had to cover her cries by kissing her deeply on the mouth. Those kisses also aroused her, possessed and conquered her. They were fierce and at the same time achingly gentle so that she was beyond thinking when he finally entered her and began to thrust inside her.

She'd been too lost in ardor to notice he'd removed his breeches. When had this happened? What else had she missed?

Oh, glory.

They were lying naked together in bed.

She ran her hands along the length of him, felt along the muscled bulges of his arms, and inhaled his manly heat.

His body was beautiful, hard and strong and lean.

Their thighs pressed together as he moved inside her with feral grace. But she would not call him delicate or graceful. This man was power and sinew. Thunder and lightning. His hands were roughened by years of battle, and she felt the scrape of his day's growth of beard along her cheek.

His desire was intense.

She felt it in the exquisite way he kissed her and made her body hum.

She saw the ravenous longing in his eyes.

But he was holding back, no doubt determined to be gentle with her. "I don't want to hurt you, love. You've never done this before."

"I know, but I think my body is ready for you." She was already entwined around him, the urge instinctive as she wrapped her legs around his hips and held on to his shoulders. "You won't hurt me, Rowan. I trust you."

She thought this knowledge would ease him, but his honed body became even more taut, and the intensity of their coupling heightened.

In turns, she closed her eyes to feel the music of their bodies as they moved in a timeless dance of love and then opened them to watch the smoky embers of his eyes as he brought the dance to its nearing end.

An odd pressure began to build inside her. "Rowan, I..."

He seemed to understand what she was feeling, this fiery heat...like a volcano about to erupt. It built and built, suddenly exploding and sending waves of liquid fire flowing through her.

"Blessed saints, Cara." He covered her noisy mouth with a searing kiss, at the same time thrusting into her more urgently, his body hot and damp as he planted himself deep and spilled his seed inside of her.

He collapsed atop her with a much-satisfied grunt, the weight of him surprisingly pleasurable.

She felt his ragged breaths as his chest pressed down on hers and heard the rapid beat of his heart pounding as fiercely as her own.

All too quickly, he pulled out of her. But it was only to roll off her and draw her into the cradle of his arms. "Gad, that was good. How do you feel, love?"

She laughed softly. "Did I leave you with any doubt? It was beyond anything I could have imagined. It was wonderful. But you knew it would be."

He grinned and kissed her on the forehead. "I hoped it would be."

"Was it truly all right for you, Rowan?"

He kissed the swell of her breast. "More than all right, love. I am in great danger of turning into a besotted fool."

They coupled again before dawn, an exquisitely intimate moment of perfection.

When the sun began to peek over the horizon, she tossed on her shift and robe while he donned breeches and a shirt, and they quietly made their way out of the cottage and headed down to the beach.

The air was warm, and the water appeared calm as they stood on the sand, holding hands while they peered across the azure expanse. "Come in with me, Cara."

He tugged gently on her hand.

She eyed the water warily.

"Still scared, love?"

She nodded. "I don't mind watching you from the shore."

He looked disappointed as he undressed.

"Drat, now you are going to make me be brave. I am not a coward but promise you won't let go of me." She took a deep breath and slipped out of her robe. However, she kept her shift on for modesty, not that it would hide anything of her body once it got wet. Nor did she feel the need for modesty around him, but what if the dolphins reappeared?

Well, those dolphins would not care what she was wearing.

Rowan emitted a hearty chuckle when she told him what had been going through her mind. "Keep your shift on, love. Your body is for my eyes alone. I am not sharing you with anyone, man or beast."

He took her hand and was beyond patient with her as they inched deeper into the water until it came up to her chest. "I'll be right beside you, Cara. Why don't you try to swim?"

"Will you swim with me?"

"Yes, love."

"All right." She thought she would have difficulty, but it took her only a few strokes to regain her ability. Soon, they were swimming side by side and it felt wonderful. She had not done up her hair, so the long strands fanned out behind her as she moved through the water.

"Can angels also be mermaids?" Rowan teased, obviously enjoying the sight of her.

"I am neither, I assure you." Certainly no mermaid when she was still too afraid to swim out where the water was over her head.

Nor did Rowan force her.

She made her way back to shore a short while later and watched as he went into deeper waters when the dolphins returned to frolic with him. She enjoyed watching him cavort with them from her spot of safety.

She was not afraid of them after watching the care they took with Rowan. But being comfortable in those deep waters was something she would have to work harder to achieve.

The memory of that violent, unforgiving sea all those years ago was not something easily overcome.

She would in time.

Especially with Rowan beside her.

It was not long before the dolphins headed back out to sea, and Rowan swam back toward her. He proudly neared the shore, his body wet and glistening as his feet planted on the sandy bottom, and the water swirled around his chest. "Did you see me ride on them, Cara?"

She was hopping with excitement. "I did! You were splendid! Neptune, god of the sea."

She waded in to meet him as he came toward her and lifted her in his arms. "Lord, you make me happy."

"The feeling is mutual, Your Grace."

He carried her back on land and used his shirt to dry her off. He laughed as she squealed when he tossed off her soaked shift and rubbed her body down. Then he helped her don her robe before tending to himself. He put on his breeches but merely slung the damp shirt over one broad shoulder.

They sat on the sand, she in his arms again so that her back was to his chest, and his arms were closed around her while they listened to the soft whoosh of the waves rushing to shore and the occasional caw of a bird hovering over the water in search of a morning meal.

He brushed her hair back and kissed her neck. "Cara, I mean it. I've never been happier. You feel so soft and perfect in my arms."

"It is this place, Moonstone Landing. The bracing salt air. The warmth of the sun. The glistening sea. This place calls to you. Like the ebb and flow of the tide…you may leave here for a while, but you always come back. It draws you back."

He kissed her again. "No, love. It is beautiful, and I hope we shall spend many summers here, but—"

"Summers with our children. Wouldn't it be wonderful?"

"Yes, with a dozen Strathmore brats crawling around us in the sand like little crabs. But let me enjoy you alone for this summer. I'll do my duty soon enough. Indeed, you may already be carrying my heir."

He kissed her yet again, his lips warm and tender against her nape. "The lure is not the village or the sea. It is you, Cara. I don't need to return here to capture the beauty. I'll always have my Moonstone angel with me. You are all I shall ever need."

He spread out his shirt beneath them, set her down on it, and proceeded to show her just how much he needed her.

Epilogue

Moonstone Landing
Cornwall, England
September 1815

ROWAN COULD HAVE returned to London the week after he and Cara had wed to deal with his sisters and Lady Yvonne. However, they were not worth the trouble. He'd dealt with his sisters by writing to their husbands and informing them of what they had done. He had no doubt those men, who relied on his good graces, would ship those wasps off to their holdings in the outer reaches of the kingdom and keep them there until his temper cooled...assuming it ever would.

As for Lady Yvonne, he had also sent word to her father reporting what she had done. Lying under oath was no small matter, and he knew her father was not the sort to let the transgression pass unpunished. He had no idea what the man would do—possibly marry her off to the first wealthy toad who came along.

The two warrant officers had offered to carry his angry word back to Lord Fortesque. He'd taken them up on the offer, knowing they could be relied upon. The pair had taken a liking to Cara, shocked when she showed them kindness. For this reason, they promised to follow Rowan's instructions to the letter. "We'll make certain the duchess's reputation is properly restored, Yer Grace."

He had written to Lord Fortesque demanding the man not merely rescind the warrant but nullify it, expunge it as though it had never been issued.

Others may think of it as a minor matter, but it was not. Cara was innocent, and gossips could be cruel. He wanted that ugly business completely struck off the books.

As for Cara, he was eager to introduce her to London society. But she was not ready yet. Not that she needed any training to walk among the elite.

She was better than all the young ladies and their years of lessons.

What she lacked was a suitable wardrobe, one that was now being made by a well-reputed seamstress who had recently closed her London shop and retired to Moonstone Landing. The woman, one Madame de Clare, had spent days going over colors, fabrics, and styles with Cara and his grandmother.

He found the chore mind-numbingly dull and managed to avoid having to give an opinion by disappearing to visit his friend, Cain St. Austell, now that he returned to his palatial estate, newly married himself to Phoebe and Chloe's sister, Lady Henley.

Cara was beaming when he strode in after settling Ares back in the stable. "Where's the seamstress?"

"Gone for the day, and she's a modiste," Cara said with a grin, throwing her arms around his neck and kissing him sweetly. "She finished with today's fittings, and we chose more fabrics for my day gowns. Your grandmother has just retired for her afternoon nap. I'm afraid you are alone with me."

"Blast, why ever would I want to be in the company of the loveliest woman on earth? What shall we do to amuse ourselves?"

He lifted her in his arms and started to carry her upstairs.

"Rowan!" she cried in a frantic whisper. "It is the middle of the afternoon. Mildred is still here. And your grandmother will hear us. Is it not bad enough we…you know…at night?"

"You are the noisy one, not me. You leave me so drained I barely manage to eke out a grunt."

She giggled. "We do have fun, don't we?"

"Yes, love. A shocking amount of it."

"Oh, you have a letter from London. It could be important."

He sighed and set her down, then took the letter off the tray atop the small table by the entryway. "It is from the Bow Street runner I retained, Homer Barrow. He is an excellent man, but I did not think even he could recover that necklace so quickly."

She sat beside him on the sofa, peering over his shoulder as they read the man's report. "I find it sadly ironic," he said with a trace of sadness, "that your three accusers were the actual thieves. I could press charges against them if I were so inclined."

"I don't want you to. Their status in society protects them from proper punishment. To prolong this sad business will only add fuel to the ugly gossip."

Rowan arched an eyebrow. "You wouldn't go after them because you do not have it in your heart to hurt others, even those who attempted to hurt you. If you have a flaw, Cara, and not that I am saying you do. Gad, you are quite wonderful and perfect. But if you did have a flaw, it would be that you are far too forgiving."

"I am no simpering fool to be trodden upon at will. I hope never to see them again, and I shall never forget what they tried to do to me. But you have punished them already by cutting off their allowance and forcing their husbands to send them not merely out of London but to some place where there is no *society* of any sort. On top of it, your grandmother intends to cut them out of any inheritance they would have received from her."

"She spoke to you about it?"

Cara nodded. "She wanted to leave their share to me, but I really do not want it or need it now that I am your wife and apparently one of the wealthiest women in Cornwall. You know my cousin, Spencer Angel, is head clerk at the local bank. I do not think the ink was dry on the hefty deposit into my account before he ran to tell me. But as for your grandmother's personal assets, we are going to select worthy charities. Orphans, injured soldiers returning from war. The sick. The elderly. There are plenty who suffer."

"I trust you and my grandmother to make the best choices." He set aside the letter and hoisted her onto his lap. "Now that we've taken care of business, I cannot think of what else to do."

She glanced down at their positions. "Seems to me, you know exactly what you wish to do, and that is to ravish me. But we cannot do it here."

He groaned. "And you do not want me to take you upstairs. Where shall I take you, my love?"

"There's always the beach."

"Ah, yes. I'm still brushing sand off my arse after last night's moonlit orgy."

She buried her face against his neck and gave a snorting laugh. "That's because you rolled off the blanket. We need a bigger blanket."

"Are you willing again tonight?"

"I can be persuaded if it is with you. It will probably be our last chance before the weather turns too cold. We'll be leaving for London next week anyway."

He sighed. "I shall behave myself until nightfall then."

AS THE SUN sank below the horizon, he led Cara down to the beach and made love to her on a blanket in the sand, beneath a bright, silver moon and a shower of stars. There was a nip to the air now, so he drew her close and warmed her with his body. They drifted off to sleep to the sound of waves lapping the shore. "I love you, Cara."

"Love you, too," she replied before they dozed off in each other's arms. "This is my best summer ever."

"Mine, too, my Moonstone angel. Mine, too."

The End

Also by Meara Platt

The Dance of Love
The Miracle of Love
The Dream of Love (novella)

DARK GARDENS SERIES
Garden of Shadows
Garden of Light
Garden of Dragons
Garden of Destiny
Garden of Angels

LYON'S DEN SERIES
The Lyon's Surprise
Kiss of the Lyon
Lyon in the Rough

THE BRAYDENS
A Match Made In Duty
Earl of Westcliff
Fortune's Dragon
Earl of Kinross
Earl of Alnwick
Pearls of Fire*
(*also in Pirates of Britannia series)
Aislin
Gennalyn
A Rescued Heart

DeWOLFE PACK ANGELS SERIES
Nobody's Angel
Kiss An Angel
Bhrodi's Angel

About the Author

Meara Platt is an award winning, USA TODAY bestselling author and an Amazon UK All-Star. Her favorite place in all the world is England's Lake District, which may not come as a surprise since many of her stories are set in that idyllic landscape, including her paranormal romance Dark Gardens series. Learn more about the Dark Gardens and Meara's lighthearted and humorous Regency romances in her Farthingale series and Book of Love series, or her warmhearted Regency romances in her Braydens series by visiting her website at www.mearaplatt.com.

Printed in Great Britain
by Amazon

50314502R00059